One Sister Too Many

Also by C. S. Adler

If You Need Me

Split Sisters

With Westie and the Tin Man

Roadside Valentine

Some Other Summer

Shelter on Blue Barns Road

In Our House Scott Is My Brother

The Magic of the Glits

One Sister Too Many

C. S. ADLER

Macmillan Publishing Company
New York

Collier Macmillan Publishers
London

With thanks to David Foster for his patient
and invaluable technical assistance

Macmillan Publishing Company
866 Third Avenue, New York, NY 10022
Collier Macmillan Canada, Inc.

First Edition
Printed in the United States of America
10 9 8 7 6 5 4 3 2 1

The text of this book is set in 12 point Baskerville.

Library of Congress Cataloging-in-Publication Data
Adler, C. S. (Carole S.)   One sister too many.
Summary: With the family thrown into a turmoil by the incessant crying of
colicky, three-month-old Meredith, only twelve-year-old Case seems to notice
that Meredith's baby sitter is behaving very oddly. Sequel to "Split Sisters."
[1. Babies—Fiction.   2. Family life—Fiction.   3. Baby sisters—Fiction.
4. Sisters—Fiction]   I. Title.   PZ7.A261450p 1989 [Fic] 88-13144
ISBN 0-02-700271-3

For my dear friend Joan Porco,
a champion in the game of life,
and one who gets much joy from it

One Sister
Too Many

·ONE·

About halfway down the tree-shaded hill on my way home from the school-bus stop, I began hearing my baby sister's screams. Not to worry. She's been screaming ever since she was born, over three months ago.

I tiptoed over the flagstone entryway, through the kitchen, to the screened porch. There was my beloved stepfather working at his drawing table. He looked funny trying to sketch and jiggle Meredith in her bouncer at the same time. The bouncer's like a stretcher on wires, and Meredith usually likes it, but today she was objecting to it strongly. She's emotional, like me, but harder on the ears.

"Surprise!" I threw my arms around Gerry. "Your favorite daughter's home at last." My greeting put Gerry off his bouncing rhythm and Meredith went from scream to howl.

"Case, I'm so glad you're home. I've spent the whole day trying to calm her down. There isn't a drop of creative juice left in my body." He sounded desperate. Gerry's finally gotten successful enough to make a living as a cartoonist, but he's also got to be the mother during the day because he's the one who

1

can work at home. Mother takes over nights. Days she works as a finance manager at a big company only a half-hour commute from Livingston, which is why we moved here last summer, even though Livingston's stuck in a built-up part of New Jersey and doesn't have any water around it like Stamford did.

"I'll jounce her for you," I told Gerry, and took over from him.

Poor guy. It hadn't been his idea to have a baby. My older sister, Jen, and I were enough for him. Not that Mother had wanted another child at forty, either. Meredith was an accident. Sometimes I think she knows it and that's why she's so furious. We can't make her happy no matter how fast we rush to feed, hold, diaper, rock, bathe or burp her. Grams advised us to just let her yell, and we tried, but that didn't work, either.

The sketch on Gerry's drawing board looked like a mouth with a monster around it. "What's that?" I asked.

"It's Meredith screaming. Funny, huh?" he clued me.

"Ummm." It didn't look funny to me, but I didn't want to hurt his feelings. The black moons under his blue eyes are making his baby face look old, and he's begun doubting his own sense of humor. Motherhood is hard on him.

"You know what you ought to do," I said. "You ought to hire a baby-sitter for Meredith and get yourself an office outside the house."

"If only!" Gerry said. "But what baby-sitter would tolerate round-the-clock screaming?"

"Maybe a deaf one?" I suggested half seriously.

A sudden silence surprised us. Meredith had switched off. I smiled at her. She's as cute as any Gerber model as soon as the red fades from her skin and her mouth rounds into a little bowknot.

"Anyway, your mother will say we can't afford it." Gerry was still chewing on the sitter idea. "Probably we can't."

So far he hadn't noticed how late I was. "Jen home yet?" I asked.

"She's got computer club or her boyfriend or something after school," Gerry mumbled. He flipped the page on his drawing pad. I saw that he'd drawn Meredith as sleeping angel and Meredith smiling.

The only time Meredith had ever smiled at me was the day she wet my pillow. It was her first month, and I was even volunteering for diaper duty just to get near her. Actually, I'd been the only one in the whole family who'd wanted a baby. Dumb, innocent me. I'd thought it would be like taking care of a live doll and daydreamed about teaching her/him to read using alphabet blocks. I guess I thought he/she would be born older.

Meredith was making outraged faces, gearing up to yell again. Quickly, I asked Gerry, "Don't you want to know how my day went?"

"However," he said, looking at me thoughtfully, "it might be worth looking into."

"My day?"

"Getting a sitter and an office somewhere. It probably *is* the only solution."

"Thompson gave me detention again, and she's

going to call you guys tonight." I heaved a mighty sigh. "She picks on me all the time, Gerry."

Grumpily he asked me, "What'd you do now?"

"Nothing. I wish you'd tell her I'm really a terrific kid."

"What'd you say to her, Case?"

Gerry was getting pretty shrewd. It's true I have a fast mouth. Before I even know it, I'm talking back, especially to outright tyrants like Mrs. Thompson. Well, suffering in silence has never been my style.

"She hates me, Gerry. Would she have given me detention *and* be calling my parents if she didn't hate me? After all, I wasn't doing drugs or cheating on a test. I just had my heels on the table. And we'd already picked our books, which is what she sent us to the library for. So how was it wrong for Willie and Andrea and me to be behind the stacks quietly discussing our project?"

"Your mother asked around about Mrs. Thompson. She's supposed to be a very good teacher."

"But too strict and she can't stand anybody different."

"Well, stop being so different," Gerry said.

Meredith came on the air again while I was trying to tell him he didn't understand. Gerry clutched his head. "Case, would you take her away for an hour? Just give me an hour to work in peace. Please!"

"Sure. Wait'll I get my earphones." I'd discovered I could mute Meredith pretty well with my Walkman and earphones.

The phone rang as I was running upstairs for

them. It was Willie Rose, my first, best and only friend in this neighborhood—in fact, in the whole seventh grade.

Willie never wastes time with hellos or good-byes. "She's at it again," he said, hearing Meredith in the background.

The way I got to be his friend was he brought his pet boa constrictor to school to show his science teacher, and the snake got loose in homeroom. Nobody would help Willie look for it but me. I found it, too, under Mrs. Thompson's desk curled up in the wastebasket.

"I'm sorry you're the only one Thompson gave detention to, Case," Willie said. He's loyal, a really steady kid, as short and chunky as me, but his cheeks are fatter, and he's a lot better student.

"Detention was nothing, Willie. What scares me is, she's calling *tonight,* which means my mother'll probably take the call."

"That does it. We better forget Tippy's party."

"Are you crazy? Why?" The farewell party for Tippy, our cute young student teacher, was the project Willie and Andrea and I had been discussing when Mrs. Thompson discovered us.

"Because you're already in enough trouble without breaking official school rules."

"It's a stupid rule," I said. "Are we sheep, Willie? Why should we obey stupid rules? It's wrong to send Tippy off without a party. At least, she *tried* to make school fun."

"Come on over and we'll discuss it," Willie said.

He won't come to my house anymore because of Meredith. Willie's an only child. Noise bothers him.

"I'll get there as soon as I can."

Willie grunted and hung up.

I went on up to my room after the earphones. Well, actually it was Jen's room, but I'd moved in with her when my room became the nursery and Meredith turned out to be such a noisy roommate. Looking around, I was glad I'd gotten there before Jen. In my frantic search for gym socks this morning, I'd dumped half the contents of my dresser onto the floor. And I hadn't had time to make my bed again. Also, my half of Jen's desk was piled with scraps of material from the purple and pink appliquéd pillow I was making Tippy. It would be a going-away present from me personally. The only cleared surface in the room was Jen's bed. She's a neatness freak.

I found my earphones under my pillow, but bumped into guess who on my way out the door. "Hi, Jen," I said, and added before she could make a survey, "I'll fix up my side of the room just like I promised, but first I have to watch the baby for Gerry."

She stood there, calm and tall as the Statue of Liberty, only prettier. Her eyes went from my bed to my dresser to the floor, and her lips tightened. It makes me feel bad when Jen's lips tighten. If only she'd let loose like Meredith and me, I could fight back, but silent suffering slays me. "Want me to pick up a few things before I leave?" I asked hopefully.

Her eyes filled with tears. Now, my fifteen-year-old sister's no weeper. So I was mystified. The room didn't look *that* much worse than usual. You know, it's weird the way things work out. Jen and I have always been so close, and I was sure sharing a room would turn us into two halves of a clamshell. I thought we'd talk all night and confide more than ever, but what we do more than ever is fight. Jen's mad at me most of the time and does all her confiding in friends—or in Mother. Mother's Jen's favorite parent. Don't ask me why. Gerry's much nicer.

To get Jen's attention off my mess, I asked, "How's Charlie?"

"Has he called yet?"

"Not as far as I know." She sounded worried, but I knew she had nothing to worry about when it came to boys. Jen's got the only perfect nose in the family. Besides that, she's good-natured and smart. Also, she blends into groups, which is something I've never even *wanted* to do.

"Jen," I said, still trying to distract her, "I need your help. Thompson's calling Mother tonight."

"Again? You're going to wind up suspended, Case."

"She was really unfair this time."

"She's always unfair according to you."

"What's wrong with you?" I asked indignantly. "I need *sympathy*."

"What for?" Jen said bitterly. "Look at this room, Case." She pushed me aside and threw herself face down on top of her bedspread. That shook me. She never lies down without folding her bedspread and laying it on a chair. Frantically, I began picking up clothes and stuffing them back into drawers.

"Don't be mad at me," I begged her. "Please, Jen. I'm cleaning up as fast as I can."

"Go away," she muttered. "Leave me alone."

Feeling wormy, I left with the earphones and ran into Gerry on his way upstairs with the baby.

"I thought you were going to help me," he accused.

"I am. I'm here."

"Good. She needs changing." He dumped Meredith into my arms and clumped back downstairs.

"Hi, Merry," I cooed at the damp little bundle in the crook of my arm. I'd nicknamed her Merry before she was born, when the parents first chose "Meredith," but so far the nickname didn't fit.

She fussed as I carried her into the nursery. "You wet and icky? Want Case to make you all nice and dry? Poop de doop, iggle de pop, gootchy gee." One-way conversations are hard. I tend to use nonsense words as filler. I sure hope Meredith doesn't understand me and think her big sister's an idiot.

She whimpered when I set her down on the towel on top of the dresser to change her. I switched to nursery rhymes to entertain her. "Little Miss Muffet sat on a tuffet . . ." It's amazing how a creature with such delicate fingers and toes, such dainty snail-shell ears, can yell so loud.

She carried on for a long five minutes after I picked her up and walked around patting her back. The only thing of mine left in the nursery was the wallpaper, which I'd picked last summer when Jen was my only sister. It had purple flowers, the wallpaper did, because purple's my favorite color. With just Meredith's crib and chest of drawers and a rocking chair in it, the room seemed big and empty.

Too bad Meredith hadn't turned out to be Merry. It would have been a lot easier to share *her* room space. She wouldn't hate me for being messy. Jen won't believe that I can't just *get* neat, that messiness is something I was born with, like dark eyes and hair and a bumpy nose. Like Meredith was born cranky.

When she quieted down again, I laid her in her crib and tied one end of my hair ribbon around her ankle and the other end to her bird mobile. I had tried that before. Smart kid; she remembered and immediately kicked her foot, not both feet, just the one with the ribbon, to make the bird mobile spin. Her eyes, blue like Gerry's, followed the birds as they flapped up and down and around above her head.

"Go to it, kid," I said. "Make it do what you want." For a while, Merry kicked, and the mobile spun. Then her eyelids closed. She fought them open, but they closed again. When they finally stayed closed, I detached the ribbon for safety's sake and covered her.

The porch, I thought, getting another of the ideas that Willie admires me for. Summer was coming. In the winter the screened porch was too cold, but it'd be a perfect place to sleep in the summer. That's what I'd do. I'd move onto the porch, and then Jen would stop giving me the silent treatment and love me again. Terrific! I hurried downstairs to tell Gerry.

·TWO·

Gerry wasn't working. He was just sitting on his stool staring at his drawing pad. I put my hand on his shoulder and said, "Another reason you've got to get an office is because I need the porch."

"What for?" he asked absentmindedly.

"Because Jen can't stand living with me. It's either move to the porch or the basement, and you don't want your beloved daughter down there in the damp with the spiderwebs and the leaky washing machine and the gas fumes from the furnace, do you?"

"You can't move to the porch, Case."

"Why not?"

"The whole family uses it, especially now that summer's coming."

"I don't mind sharing."

"Your mother sits out here when she's relaxing."

"You mean five minutes on a Sunday afternoon? I'll leave when she wants it."

"Your sister came out here to neck with Charlie the other night. She's at an age where she needs her privacy."

I was shocked. "Necking! That's a disgusting

expression. Jen doesn't neck, or make out, or do anything gross."

"What's gross at twelve is normal at fifteen. Kissing's okay, so long as that's as far as it goes, and Jen's a sensible girl."

"Well, so am I."

"You? No." He gave me a one-armed hug. "You're too passionate."

"Nobody in this family appreciates me," I complained, "not even you. Here I come up with this great idea about how you can get your work done—"

"Forget it. I checked out your mother's budget plan. There's no extra bucks."

"But, Gerry, if you don't earn any money because you can't get your work done, that'll wreck the budget worse, won't it?"

He considered and began nodding. "Not a bad argument."

"So then, can I move to the porch? Just my bed and my little little dresser?"

"You'll have to ask your mother." He always passes the buck when I get tough because Mother's tougher.

"That's not fair," I said.

"What's not fair?" Mother asked. She was standing in the doorway. This morning Mother'd gone off to work in a boxy suit to hide her extra weight and a full makeup job to hide her tiredness. The suit was still working, but the makeup wasn't. The same black moons Gerry had were under her eyes, probably from staying up nights with Meredith.

11

Before I could answer Mother, Gerry asked her, "Hard day?"

"Hectic. How about you?"

"Terrible. If I don't come through with the work I promised them, my publisher will start looking for another cartoonist, but how can I work with Meredith yelling all day? All I got done was two loads of wash."

"She's quiet now," Mother observed.

"Case got her to sleep."

I perked up to receive Mother's praise, but she slumped and said wearily, "I guess she'll be up all night again, then."

"Tell me the truth, Marian." Gerry aimed his thumb at his sketch. "Is this funny?"

Mother studied the sketch. "A creature from outer space?" she asked.

Gerry moaned and flipped pages to show her the sleeping and smiling sketches of Meredith.

"Well," Mother said, "it might be funny to some-one who doesn't have a colicky baby."

"Case thinks I should get an office outside the house," Gerry said.

"*Does* she!" Mother's emphasis made me cringe.

"It would be cheaper to hire a baby-sitter and rent an office than for me not to earn anything," Gerry pointed out.

Mother's left eyebrow rose up to her hairline. "We'll talk about it later," she said.

She doesn't believe in arguing in front of the children—which is how last year Jen and I never knew they were separating until it happened. The things I tried to get them reattached! I nearly killed myself. I mean really. It wasn't just that I wanted both my parents in one place; it was that my mother actually split Jen and me apart. She moved to New York with Jen and left me to go-it-alone with Gerry. That's Mother for you. But my credit for getting them back together again got used up fast, thanks to Mrs. Thompson's phone calls, which began last September. Now I didn't dare mention the porch. In the mood she was in, Mother would zap the idea before I got it out of my mouth. Besides, Mrs. Thompson was due to call soon. Double zap and out.

"Has anybody started dinner yet?" Mother asked.

"I'll make the salad," I offered sweetly.

Jen traipsed into the kitchen while I was washing the red-leafed lettuce. She stopped next to the wall telephone and asked me wistfully, "Charlie hasn't called, has he?"

"Don't worry. He will."

"What makes you think so?"

"He's got to know how lucky he is to have you," I said, but she slumped into a chair, unconvinced. No matter how often I tell her she's perfect, Jen keeps underrating herself. If anybody ever told *me* I was perfect, I'd be happy to believe them.

"Mother looks really tired. So I told her I'd make the salad," I said. "Hint, hint, hint."

"I'll do the rest of the dinner," Jen offered as I'd hoped. She got up to check out what we had in the refrigerator.

"What'd you and Charlie fight about?"

"He wants me to go steady."

"So? That's good, isn't it?"

"Case, you don't understand, and I don't want to talk about it."

"We used to be so close," I complained. "Don't you remember how close we were? But ever since *boys* got into your life, you won't share with me anymore."

"I can't share with a messy twelve-year-old," Jen said.

That hurt. "I can't help being twelve," I said. "I can't help being messy, either."

Jen's cheeks flushed with anger. "You can, too, help. You can reform and clean up after yourself like you promised."

"I try, but mess just happens to me, Jen. Before I even know it, it happens."

My plea didn't move her the way it would have before boys, before Meredith, before she'd grown up and away from me so suddenly. She turned on the silent treatment. I'd rather be yelled at any day than undergo the silent treatment.

The conversation at our dinner table that night was not inspiring. Mostly it was about whether Meredith's formula could be what was wrong with her, that it might be too rich or not rich enough. Meanwhile, Jen and I both eyed the phone anxiously. When it did ring, we nearly knocked each other down getting to it. Jen, no doubt, hoped it would be Charlie. Me, I was going to tell Mrs. Thompson my parents were out, at a funeral, in the hospital, gone forever and unavailable to talk to her. . . . It was Willie Rose.

14

"When are you coming over?"

"Now," I said, suddenly realizing my best move was to be gone when the Thompson phone call came.

"Do I have to do the dishes?" I asked the parents after I hung up. "I made the salad and set the table."

"I'll do the dishes," Mother said. Just then Meredith went off like a fire alarm. "I thought infants were supposed to sleep twenty hours a day," Mother said. "Meredith doesn't sleep more than two."

"The doctor said she'd grow out of it by three months," Gerry said.

Mother sighed. "She doesn't know that rule, either."

Merry and I don't go by the rules, I was going to say, but I thought better of it and slipped out the door instead.

Our backyard and Willie's connect at the corner where a huge old hickory tree grows. Last spring I carved Willie's initials and mine inside a heart on that tree, which embarrassed him so much that he avoided me for a week. It was hard convincing him that I hadn't adopted him as my boyfriend, that hearts just happen to be my hallmark.

Willie's mother opened the front door when I rang the bell. She always greets me warily, the way people who don't like dogs act when one approaches them. It must still bother her to have her son's best friend be a girl. She'd questioned Willie about that, he'd told me. Also, he told me that his parents don't like kids much. He suspects they only like him because he's their son.

"Hi," I called to Mr. Rose, who was hiding behind

15

his newspaper. He just grunted in return as I passed through the living room. The Roses have a furniture store. Talking to people all day must use up their stock of friendliness.

The sign on Willie's door says KNOCK BEFORE ENTERING. I knocked and walked on in.

"Something's wrong with the thermostat in the lizard's box," Willie said. "I changed the bulb in the lamp, but that's not it." Willie's plump cheeks are rosy. He's got big brown eyes and a little nose, and I think he's kind of cute, even if he is built like an ice cube.

I got Zeus, the boa constrictor that first brought us together, out of his glass box. Willie says Zeus likes to be petted, so I always get that over with first. Not that I mind stroking his smooth, dry skin, but Zeus is so lazy he's boring. While I sat on the bed with him, I looked around.

Willie's room's a zoo. His parents buy him whatever he wants, which happens to be animals, small ones. The walls of his room are stacked chin high with terrariums, aquariums and cages. His bookshelves hold bags of cedar chips and fish food. Willie lives on the bed. At least, he sleeps and does his homework there. All his clothes and junk are in a walk-in closet. The room doesn't smell too much, because Willie's mother bought him a big fan and he keeps the windows open, also because he's very conscientious about changing the litter and food in the cages.

My favorite of Willie's animals is a cute little golden-haired guinea pig. Willie named it Dracula because it bit him when he was trying to think of a name for it. After a minute, I draped Zeus back over his branch in his climate-controlled terrarium and took out Dracula. Well, he's never bitten me.

Willie was concentrating on his tinkering. He's happiest poking at some malfunctioning electrical device in what he calls his "habitats."

"Willie, I need your brain," I said. The silly-looking dust mop of a guinea pig was climbing all over me, wriggling its nose and showing its buckteeth as it explored my pocket.

"You've got a good one of your own," Willie said.

"But I can't think of a way to convince my mother to let me move onto the porch." Of course, Willie wanted to know why I wanted to move onto the porch, but all I had to say was "Jen" to make him understand.

"Thompson hasn't talked to your folks yet, has she?" Willie asked.

"No."

"Once she talks to them, they might make you move out altogether. Tell you what. I'll ask my folks if you can have our guest room."

"Fun-ny," I said. Not everyone understands Willie's sense of humor. "This really is a problem, Willie. It kills me to have Jen mad at me. She's important to me."

"More important than The Screamer?" Willie calls Meredith The Screamer without much affection. I've pointed out to him that she's a small animal like all the ones he collects, but he can't see her that way. Maybe he takes after his parents in not liking children.

17

"I'm the wrong person to talk to in this case," Willie said. "I wouldn't want to room with you, either."

"Willie!" I protested. "Would you hate someone for not hanging up her clothes instantly? You put up with poopy hamsters and dead guppies and gerbils that eat their own babies."

"That's different. Animals can't help themselves, but you can. All you have to do is get neat."

"That's like telling a tone-deaf person to practice his scales so he can be an opera star."

"Well," he said thoughtfully, "you could wear earplugs and move in with The Screamer if you're really desperate."

He had that little quirk at the corner of his lip that meant he was joking, but I took his idea seriously. With my Walkman and the earphones, it just might work. "You know what I can do," I said. "I'll tell Mother she's got to let me sleep on the porch or else I'll move in with the baby."

"So? She'll let you move in with the baby."

"Oh, Willie, just because I told you Mother prefers Jen doesn't mean she *hates* me."

Willie flicked the thermostat with his finger. "There," he said, "that does it."

"Let's talk about Tippy's party now," I said.

Willie fixed me with his earnest brown eyes. "Case, for once, will you listen to me and forget that party? It'll get you in more trouble than it's worth."

"Since when have I ever stopped doing something that's right because it might get me in trouble?"

Willie ignored my question. He said, "You're giving Tippy the pillow, and I'll give her the scrapbook with the class's pictures like you said—I've got it mostly done already—and that's enough for her."

"You're not quitting on me, are you, Willie? Not you!" I was so upset, I sat up too fast, and Dracula fell off my shoulder. He got scared and scuttled under the bed.

"We better get him out before he poops," Willie said.

While Willie put on a leather glove to protect his fingers from Dracula's fangs, I bellied down to the floor and reached under the bed, but Dracula kept his distance. Soon I could see Willie's gloved hand on the other side of the bed, then his big brown eyes and plump cheeks. Dracula huddled against the wall midway between us.

"I just don't see why you should get in trouble for somebody who isn't even a friend of yours," Willie said from his side of the bed. "We'll probably never see Tippy again, and even if she does come back, it won't be to see us especially. *We're* not her favorites."

"What kind of attitude is that? That's a rotten attitude. She's nice, so it's nice to do something nice to show her we appreciate how nice she is."

"Well, you can't have the party in the school. So where are you going to hold it?"

"I have an idea about that."

"You always have an idea."

I rolled away from the bed and sat up. "I thought you thought my ideas were great."

"Sometimes. What's this one?"

"We'll have the party after school on the picnic tables behind the cafeteria. Anybody can use those tables; so we won't be breaking any rules."

"What if it rains?"

"It won't."

Willie shook his head. "I don't like it. Why do you always have to go against everything?"

"I don't go against everything, just things that don't make any sense."

"I don't know," Willie said. "Sometimes you go too far. Like Thompson today. You could've taken your feet off the table when you saw her, and you didn't have to talk back to her."

"I *didn't* talk back to her.

"You sounded like it. . . . You said, 'We're having a private discussion and aren't bothering anybody.'" It was a good imitation of me.

"Well, that was the truth, wasn't it?"

"But it sounded like you were smart-mouthing her. She asked what we were doing. You could have just said, 'We've picked our books and are waiting for the end of the period, Mrs. Thompson.'"

"Picky, picky." He was annoying me. "Why didn't *you* answer her, then?"

"I would've if you'd given me a chance."

Dracula picked that instant to make a dash for freedom. As he ran past my fingers, I snatched him and dumped him back in his cage. "You'll help me with the party, won't you?" I asked Willie, who got up from the floor.

"I guess so," he said. "But don't tell the class yet. They'll talk about it, and Thompson or the principal will get wind of it, and we'll both be in trouble."

"Okay," I agreed. "I'll do the invitations, and we'll hand them out a couple of days before Tippy has to leave us. How's that?"

"Not good, but better than nothing. Now can we play Scrabble?"

As he was getting his super deluxe Scrabble edition down from the shelf in his closet, I thought over Willie's criticism. It bothered me because he's always admired me for being bold, and I need his admiration.

"You know, Willie," I said as he handed me two metal pegs and a plastic tile holder, "you're not much of a regular guy yourself."

"That's true," he said calmly, without letting me explain that he isn't regular because he's more interested in animals than people and hates sports besides.

"Well, so why're you picking on *me*?" I asked.

"Because you stick out more. I'm different, but I don't stick out like you do, Case. I mean, you *make* yourself stick out."

I thought of the Swedish sailor suit I'd worn to school the first day last fall. I did stick out deliberately sometimes. I'd rather be original than an assembly-line kid. "I can't help it. It's my nature."

"Like being neat?" He asks these stinging questions with a straight face. Mr. Innocent.

"Umm." I looked him in the eye, daring him to argue.

Instead, he offered me the bag of letter tiles. I went first. Without even thinking about it, I made a seven-letter word—science.

"Wow!" Willie said. If anyone was going to make

21

a seven-letter word, it was usually him.

"That's okay," I said glumly. "You'll beat me, anyway."

Somehow I felt bad. It seemed to me that nobody in my life liked me as much as I liked them, and nobody I didn't like liked me at all. Well, being popular's never mattered to me. I just wished I had something to fall back on besides people, like Willie had his animals. . . . "Maybe I ought to get a guinea pig," I said out loud.

Willie didn't even blink. "It'd probably bite the baby," he said, and put down a word for thirty-six points.

He was right. "Besides, where would we fit it in our house?" I said, and sighed windily.

Willie won the Scrabble game. Even with seven-letter-word starts, I couldn't win.

I would have gone home still feeling rotten, except before I left, I asked Willie, "So I guess you don't like me all that much anymore, huh?"

He squinched his face up in disgust. "You know I like you," he said, so positively that my spirits soared. At least I had a friend I could count on, and if he felt like criticizing me, well, that was okay, so long as he meant it for my own good.

·THREE·

I walked home the long way around the block because I needed time to think myself over. It was past eight, and all that was left of the sun was a pink glow behind the dark trees; so it surprised me to see five-year-old Jason still out riding a trike in his driveway.

"Hi, Case," Jason called. He and I are buddies. Well, nobody else near his age lives on our street. All the three- and four-bedroom houses with porches and big yards are wasted on adults who only come outside to drive away in the morning and disappear into their garages at night.

Jason wanted me to admire his new tricycle. It was a souped-up model with psychedelic trim. "Neat," I told him. I'd baby-sat for Jason once when Jen got sick. Jason's parents prefer Jen because she's older, but Jason says he prefers me. See why he's my friend?

"I got it for my birthday," Jason said proudly. "The only thing is, it doesn't turn too good, and my mom won't let me ride it in the street."

With a driveway as short as Jason's, that was a real problem. "I'll show you how to make it turn," I offered.

I'm only five two, but even so my knees stuck out like turkey wings on the trike. Still, I was giving Jason a fair demonstration of how to ride in circles when a car passed. My luck that it was packed with girls from my class.

"Aren't you big enough for a two-wheeler yet, Case? Who's your boyfriend?" they jeered at me.

Before I could yell back, they were gone. It depresses me to be teased by people who don't like me, and the kids here in Livingston don't. It started when I tried to make an impression on the first day of school last fall. I wanted them to think I was interesting, not just another boring kid they didn't need to get to know; so I wore an outfit I'd bought in an army-navy store, a Swedish sailor shirt and a sailor hat with a pompon. The shirt was wool, and it was a hot day, and I perspired, and people kept edging away from me. They're still edging away, all except Willie Rose. Usually it doesn't bother me, but tonight being mocked by those girls in the car shook me, maybe because it came right on top of Willie's criticism and Jen's being mad at me.

Jason tried his tricycle and managed the turn this time. He thanked me.

"Anytime," I told him. "I'm pretty good on skateboards, too."

"My mom won't let me get a skateboard. When are you going to play the fishpond game with me again, Case?"

"Soon," I promised just as his mother stuck her head out the door and called him in.

I only had two more driveways to pass before I got home, but I lingered under a friendly tree that featured a slice of moon through a hole in its branches. I was feeling bad. Sure, I'm proud of being a nonconformist, but I wished more people liked me. The wish caught me by surprise. "Shame on you," I told myself. Probably it was that I'd be a teenager on my next birthday. That had to be what was softening me up.

But why *shouldn't* people like me? I'm a good person. I'm friendly and helpful, and unlike Willie who won't play ball unless some gym teacher makes him, I'm even a decent soccer, softball and volleyball player. Willie awes kids because he's a top student, but I'm average. I go from C+ to A−, depending on how much I like the teacher. Except for the day when I freaked kids out with my sailor outfit, I even *look* passably normal. Then why don't they choose me for their teams or ask me to sit with them at lunch?

Halt, I told myself, remembering Andrea. I *was* being chosen. Andrea had moved into our class two weeks ago. She'd latched onto Willie and me just as if we were a pair of winners, and she's an attractive person. Of course, she may suddenly realize her mistake and drop us.

"Don't be so negative, stupid," I told myself, and let go of the tree trunk and made it past another driveway.

The pink and red azaleas were gloriously lit by lamps along the walk of the house next to ours. Only slivers of light showed through our windows behind the overgrown bushes. I'd go talk to Jen. But she'd say I don't understand. Well, I would if she'd explain the stuff about boys to me. And suppose I could turn neat overnight; what difference would it make? When I was a messy *little* kid, she'd liked being with me. It wasn't my fault she didn't have time for me anymore.

Now that I thought about it, nobody in my family was too fond of me lately. Mother's always found fault with me. Nothing new in that. But Gerry and I used to be a pair. He'd really wanted my company the month he and I had lived on a cabin cruiser after Mother took Jen to live in New York City. Also, he and Mother had been truly grateful when I got them un-separated *and* kept Grams out of their hair while they had a love-in on the boat. That had been really nice of me because Grams is a very prickly and opinionated lady.

Probably Gerry still loves me a lot. He's just tied up in knots because Meredith's so rotten. And they really need me, even if I'm not a lovable little kid anymore. No need to rush into making myself over so long as somebody besides me likes me as is.

I walked around to the back of the house and let myself into the kitchen. The racy sounds of one of Gerry's TV cops and robbers shows came from the living room. I tiptoed past the phone toward the stairs. Whatever their reaction to Thompson's phone call, I didn't feel like dealing with it tonight.

Out from the dark of the porch came Mother's voice. "Case? Is that you?"

Caught. My stomach slithered. I squared my

shoulders and answered bravely, "Yes, Mother."

"Okay. Just checking."

I waited for the attack. Nothing. Hadn't Thompson called yet? It was close to ten. She wouldn't call this late. She must have forgotten. Could she have? Not her. More likely she'd had a car accident on the way home and was stuck in a hospital room without a phone. It had to be something at least that bad to stop Thompson from doing her duty.

Relaxed, I got curious about what Mother was doing on the porch in the dark. "Ah-ha!" I pounced, peering through the open door. "You're smoking."

"Ummm." Mother didn't even turn her head my way.

"What's the matter with you? I didn't even know you smoked."

"I never have, but I've never had a baby who won't stop crying, either," Mother said.

I switched on the lamp. My strong, no-nonsense mother was crying. I couldn't believe it. "Meredith'll stop eventually," I consoled her. "Before she gets to school, even. Nobody'll like her if she cries."

"She makes me feel so inadequate," Mother said.

"Hey! You've been a mother twice before. Remember?"

"Not a very good one. I'm not doing my job well in any direction, Case, not even at work. I put the wrong figure on a chart today, and my boss made some comment about maternity leave. No boss has ever accused me of not giving my all to a job before."

"You're just tired." I tried to comfort her. "All

you need's a good night's sleep." That was one of Grams's favorite lines.

"Come here, Case," Mother said. When I perched on the arm of her chair, she reached up and hugged me. "Thanks for the sympathy."

I sat hugging her back in surprise. I couldn't even remember the last time we'd hugged each other. It was a miracle, like getting the seven-letter word at the start of the Scrabble game, but better. "Are you letting Gerry hire a baby-sitter and move in to an office?" I asked.

"We're going to try it," Mother said. "Maybe we can't afford it, but I had to admit *I* couldn't manage if it were me trying to work at home."

Having Mother confide in me cheered me up. I felt so good I even decided to try to talk Mrs. Thompson out of calling my parents after all. I'd get down on my knees. I'd plead with her. Well, something like that.

Jen was doing her homework in our bedroom. To keep from disturbing her, I quietly took off my clothes and put everything in the hamper in the bathroom. Then I took a shower and rolled into bed, which was easy because I hadn't bothered to make it that morning. Tomorrow, I'd make it.

"Jen," I couldn't resist announcing, "I'm reforming. Really, I am this time."

She turned around to look at me. Her slim-line face was pulled down every which way with sadness. "Charlie's asked Chrissie for a date. He says he can't mean very much to me if I won't go steady with him."

"That's stupid," I said. "It's more likely you don't mean very much to him if he's going with somebody else just like that."

Jen squealed.

"Hey," I said. "If he doesn't love you, and you don't want to go steady with him, what's the problem? You should be glad it's over."

"Oh, Case, shut up. You don't understand anything."

Immediately, I was plunged back into misery. I should have mentioned moving onto the porch to Mother when she was hugging me, but I'd been too dazed to think of it. Tomorrow I'd have to tackle both Mrs. Thompson and Mother.

"I'm sorry," Jen said unexpectedly. "I shouldn't have snapped at you, but I feel so rotten."

"That's okay. I'm sorry you feel bad," I said, perking up. "I guess we all got depressed tonight. Mother, too."

Jen was wiping her face with tissues. She said, "That's because our grandmother called. She's worried about Meredith's colic. Grams says if Mother stayed home and took care of her, Meredith wouldn't scream all the time. Mother got upset, and Gerry took the phone away and said he was a very good mother, and Grams should mind her own business. He's never been rude to Grams before. Meredith's making us all nervous wrecks."

"She's a terror, all right," I said absently. I was thinking. Last summer when Grams came to rescue Gerry and Mother's marriage, and I dragged her off for a week alone with me in New York City, we'd become friends. I'd even promised her I'd visit her in Cincinnati sometime. I hadn't yet.

"Jen, I said, "if Meredith's still screaming this summer, would you want to go visit Grams with me?"

"Not me," Jen said.

"Why not?"

"Because all my friends belong to the swim club, and Mother says we can join. I'm going to take diving lessons from Charlie."

"Charlie? The same Charlie you're not going steady with?"

"He's going to be a lifeguard at the pool. I like him a lot, Case, even if I won't let him have what he wants."

"You mean going steady with him?"

"Case, going steady around here means doing more than just kissing."

"Oh," I said. It was finally clear to me. "Oh, boy!"

"I've got to finish this chapter for a test tomorrow," Jen said. "Could you?"

"Sure," I said, and closed my eyes.

No sooner had I begun to doze off, than I heard Meredith tuning up for her nightly howl. Earphones from the Walkman, plus music, tuned her out just fine from the next bedroom down the hall. If Mother wouldn't let me try the porch, I'd move into Meredith's room after school. That should show Jen how important she is to me.

I wondered how long it would take Gerry to find a sitter. If he found a really good one, it might turn us into a happy family again. I hoped he'd find somebody as young and cute as my student teacher, someone fun to be around. I'd be the one who was home with her most because I got home from school early, and Gerry would be away at his office. She'd like me, of course, and together we'd tame Meredith.

"Case is wonderful with babies," she'd tell my parents.

"Case is a wonderful kid," they'd say. And summer would come, and Jen and I would spend a lot of time at the pool together. Maybe I could even help her with Charlie. I'd make him realize how lucky he was to have her so crazy about him. I fell asleep smiling. It never even occurred to me that a baby-sitter could be bad news rather than good, or that my life could be on its way from bad to worse.

·FOUR·

Thursday was not the greatest day of the year for me. It didn't start well. It didn't end well. And the middle rotted.

I was hanging out the bedroom window, inhaling the May morning smell of hyacinths and wet grass, when I heard Jen yell, "Case, did you take my socks?"

"Me?" I stalled for time. "Aren't they in your drawer?"

"No, they aren't. What'd you do with them?"

It irked me that she was so sure of my guilt; so I said sweetly, "Your drawer is full of socks, all neatly folded in rows, but you can have any you want from my dresser."

"I was saving those white socks for gym. I bet they're in your gym bag, or did you lose them already?"

Jen's eyes squinch up and her mouth goes thin when she's angry. She looked fierce, but I kept my cool. "They're *not* in my gym bag." They weren't. But I suddenly remembered where they were. In my school locker. I'd meant to bring them home, wash them by hand, stick them in the dryer and slip them back into Jen's drawer, folded so she'd never know I'd borrowed them. Unfortunately, getting detention made me forget.

"You *know* I bought those socks with my baby-sitting money," Jen said.

I felt like a rat, but I insisted. "You could have lost them, or somebody else could have borrowed them. Why are you so sure it's me?"

"Because Meredith's feet are too small. Gerry's are too big. And Mother doesn't wear socks."

"Well, but you don't have to treat me like a criminal. You're hurting my feelings, Jen."

"You did take them, didn't you?"

I squirmed and confessed, "I did, but not today."

"Where are they?"

"See, I knew you wouldn't want me slaughtered by my gym teacher, and you didn't have gym yesterday, but I did."

"Did you bring them home?"

I shook my head in silent shame.

She growled at me. My queenlike sister actually growled and showed her teeth. How could she get so mad over a pair of socks? "You are a stinker, Case," she said. "You are a real, rotten stinker."

"Jen!" I pleaded, but she grabbed a pair of socks from her drawer and slammed out of the room. I think they were pink, the socks—one of several pairs that used to be white before Gerry washed them with Mother's red nightgown. I hoped Jen's gym teacher would be understanding. Probably she would. Jen never got in trouble.

I started to make my bed, but then Meredith was crying, and Mother rushed into my room with a bottle. "Case, could you feed the baby? Gerry's out jogging, and I have to get ready for work."

"Sure." I was hoping that Jen would leave for school without telling Mother what a rotten sister I was. Before Jen did me in, and before the fateful phone call came from Thompson, I'd put in my pitch for the porch.

I bent over Meredith's crib, waving the bottle at her. "Nice, warm, delicious milk," I said. "Yummy yum-yum." She screamed as if I were offering her poison. "Okay." I picked her up. "So you don't want breakfast. You don't have to scream about it." She was sopping. Why did I always get stuck with diaper duty?

Meredith stiffens up when she's into power yelling, which makes it hard to change her diaper. I did my best, even powdering her little round bottom, but she wasn't comforted.

"Why aren't you giving her her bottle?" Mother demanded to know. She was buttoning her blouse in the doorway.

"She needed changing first."

"Okay, hand her over. Thanks, Case." Mother sat down in the rocker, cradling the baby, and Merry finally decided she was hungry. Since she couldn't suck and scream at the same time, she got blissfully quiet.

I was still in my pajamas. "You'd better get dressed," Mother said, "or you'll be late for school."

"Mother mine, I need your help," I began, and

told her all about how I was getting on Jen's nerves and how rooming together was destroying our relationship. "About all I can do is move onto the porch," I said. "It's not ideal, but I'm willing because I can't stand having Jen mad at me."

"You're not moving onto the porch," Mother said.

"Why? I'll just use a small corner for my bed and chest. I won't get in anybody's way."

"No," Mother said.

"No, what? No, you agree I won't get in anybody's way?"

"No, you can't move onto the porch."

I waited for her to offer reasons that I could knock down, but she sat calmly feeding Meredith. A plain no is hard to budge. I swallowed and said as pitifully as I could, "I don't know why I try to be helpful around here when nobody ever tries to be helpful to me."

"Come on, Case," Mother said. "I'd say you're pretty well cared for. You look as if you eat enough, and you've got plenty of clothes, although no one could guess that by the way you dress."

"Food, clothing and shelter aren't all there is to life, Mother," I pointed out.

I thought it was a good line, but she just screwed her mouth to one side and raised an eyebrow at me. I tried my desperation plan. "The only place I can move, if you won't let me on the porch, is Meredith's room."

"So move to Meredith's room."

"Mother!" I was shocked. "Don't you love me at all?"

"What do you mean?" she asked me. "It was your idea."

I slunk off to Jen's bedroom in defeat and began searching through my clothes for something to wear to school. It was Mother's fault that I didn't have time to finish making my bed.

Ten minutes later, I leaped aboard the school bus an inch ahead of the closing door. "Gotcha," I said to the school bus driver. His game is to pretend not to see me coming and take off without me.

"Siddown," he said, with his toothpick still clenched in his teeth.

Andrea beckoned me to a seat beside her. Usually I sit with Willie, but I didn't think he'd miss my talking in his ear one morning. I waved at him and swung onto the seat beside Andrea.

Andrea's slim, with olive skin and long black hair and a very serious expression. She'll probably grow up to be beautiful. Probably Willie and I won't. It's hard to get to beautiful from chunky and plain.

"I figured out how we can do Tippy's party," I said. "If we have it on the patio after school, they can't get us for breaking the rules. Anybody can use the picnic tables on the patio after school lets out."

"Fine, sure," Andrea said without interest. Next she grabbed my arm and said intensely, "Case, you know the seventh-grade party? A boy asked me to go to it."

"That's nice. Are you going?"

"Oh, yes! If you'll go, too. My mother won't let me go alone."

"Well, I guess I might go."

"With Willie?" she asked eagerly.

"No, with me. It doesn't have to be boy-girl. You can go by yourself and play games and eat."

"But this boy asked me to go with him," she insisted. "First he asked if I could dance, and when I said yes, then he asked me."

"What boy?"

She named a kind of ordinary kid I'd never paid much attention to. I couldn't see what she was making such a fuss about.

"I've never been asked out on a date before, Case."

"Oh," I said. "Oh." Now I understood. It wasn't the boy; it was being asked out that was so great. It proved she had sex appeal. In seventh grade, sex appeal's pretty rare. In fact, even though I didn't plan to date or get involved with boys until I was in college, Andrea's having it made me feel inferior to her.

Wistfully, I said, "That's nice, Andrea. It's good you know how to dance."

"Do you?"

"Oh, sure. My dad taught my sister and me."

"Then make Willie take you. The four of us could double-date. It'll be a lot of fun."

My first date a double date! The idea went up in neon lights, but I grabbed hold of reality and said, "I couldn't make Willie do that."

"But he likes you. He doesn't like anybody else much, but he likes you."

Up to now, Andrea had been a quiet shadow who followed Willie's and my lead. I couldn't even tell if she was smart. Suddenly she'd revealed herself as that wise owl the animals bring their problems to in little kids' books. How had she caught on to what I'd missed? Willie liked me. Only me. And he was male. That had to count in my sex appeal rating. But did Willie like me enough to take me to a dance? I didn't see him as dating material, not even double-dating to a seventh-grade party.

"Well," I said to Andrea, "I guess it wouldn't hurt to ask him."

I already saw possible spin-offs from having a date. For one thing, it would impress Jen. She and Mother might even decide I'd matured enough to be in on their bathroom conferences. Fine, but how was I going to get Willie to cooperate? I couldn't bribe him, because I didn't have anything he wanted. I couldn't blackmail him, because he was too good.

I was still concentrating on the problem after homeroom when Tippy called the class to order. She was finally getting to teach us a lesson all by herself. Mrs. Thompson wasn't even sitting in back of the room watching, the way she had been up to now.

Poor Tippy. She was wearing a cotton jersey dress that showed off her curves and big white button earrings the size of her big round blue eyes, and she was sparkling with enthusiasm.

"Alone at last!" she squealed, and clapped her hands. Her smile disappeared when the boys began to whistle. Well, she'd picked a funny line to start off with, but they didn't have to make so much of it. They whistled and stamped, and the class clown stood up and held his arms out as if she might run into them.

"Here I am, Tippy."

It wasn't respectful. We weren't even supposed to call her Tippy in class. We'd all promised not to when she'd confided her nickname to us.

"Settle down now. Stop that," Tippy said. She looked scared, close to tears from the wet look of her eyes.

I jumped up and yelled at the boys, "Hey, you turkeys, do you want to get her in trouble?"

Now they were hooting and hollering at me, and guess who picked this minute to walk in? Right. Mrs. Thompson.

"That's it," she told me when she'd hauled me out to the hall without letting me explain. "I didn't call your parents last night, because something unexpected came up, but you may be sure they'll hear from me today. They'd better both come in to discuss your outrageous behavior."

"But—" was all I got to say before she ordered me down to the principal's office and stamped back inside the classroom. Everyone in there was very quiet now.

I trudged straight to the office, too depressed even to dawdle over bulletin board displays on the way. Tippy would set Mrs. Thompson straight, but she'd sure laid me low.

I sprawled on the bench where wrongdoers were stashed until the principal got around to them. The papers on desks and counters were levitating in the light breeze blowing through the open windows of the principal's office. He wasn't at his desk. Too bad. Whenever Mrs. Thompson hauls me in there to complain about my behavior, Mr. Hayes listens quietly and nods a lot, but I get the feeling he's sort of on my side. Mostly he lets me off with a lecture, a short one, and says I ought to try harder to get along with Mrs. Thompson. I do try. I can't help it that I infuriate her.

The secretary at the desk behind the fenced-off, paperwork part of the office said, "You here again, Case?"

"Only temporarily," I said. "It's a misunderstanding. I'll be sprung as soon as our student teacher tells Mrs. Thompson what really happened."

"You mouth off to her again?"

"No way. She just has it in for me."

"If you'd act more ladylike, you'd get in less trouble," the secretary advised me kindly. I was sprawled on the bench with my legs out, is what she meant.

I restrained myself from telling her that being twelve was hard enough without acting like a lady besides. She'd be sure to consider that mouthy. She returned to the list she was checking.

I studied my purple sneakers. They were growing holes over the toes, especially the big toes, but they matched my purple jeans and purple striped shirt. I don't know why Mother doesn't think I dress well. I certainly match things. Well, it's easy since most of my clothes are purple. Why more people don't like the color, I don't know. Nature's full of beautiful purple things. I was entertaining myself by naming them—crocus and hyacinths, lilacs, pansies and asters and plums, grapes and eggplants, iris, the sunset after the red starts fading, amethyst, grackles, some butterflies and bugs—when Mrs. Thompson appeared, frown first as usual. Mrs. Thompson's double-dent frown is her most prominent feature. It fits between her suspicious brown eyes. She's not a bad-looking lady when she smiles, but she only smiles at the principal and two or three favorite students. She's never smiled at me.

"Well?" Mrs. Thompson asked. Her arms were folded as if she dared me to defend myself.

"I was just trying to help Tippy," I said.

"Miss Carter, you mean. Yes, so I've been told. Why is it, Case, that everything you do, even when it's well-intentioned, is disruptive?"

"Bad luck?"

"There you go again, smart-mouthing me! That's why I still intend to see your parents. Your attitude has got to change."

My jaw dropped. How unfair could she be? She knew I hadn't done anything wrong, but she was calling my parents in, anyway. And if I protested, she'd hold that against me. The lady really hated my guts.

All the way home on the bus, Willie tried to console me. "Listen," he said, "I'll explain to your mother that you're innocent so she won't be mad at you."

"She'll be mad just because she has to take time

off from work again. She grounded me for a month last fall when Thompson made her come in."

"That day when you walked around barefoot?"

"My sneakers were too tight, Willie. And it was hot and my feet swelled."

"Hey, I'm on your side," he said.

Andrea leaned across the aisle. "Did Case ask you yet, Willie?"

"Ask me what?"

"No!" I shouted at her. I hadn't forgotten Willie's reaction to the heart I carved in the tree. I didn't want him deserting me now. I shook my head violently at Andrea to warn her not to mention the stupid party. Fortunately, Willie was looking her way instead of at me.

"We still need balloons even if we do Tippy's party outside," I said, to steer Andrea away from the double-date deal and distract Willie. "All purple ones because Tippy likes purple just like me."

Willie groaned.

"Do you think your mother would bring the soda over after school on the day of the party?" I asked Andrea. Her mother was practically the only mom I knew who didn't work.

"I think so," Andrea said.

"You're crazy," Willie told me. "You're in so much trouble already. Why even think about getting in more?"

"Just do the scrapbook like you promised," I said. "I'll do the invitations and the decorations. And Andrea, will you be in charge of refreshments?"

"Okay," Andrea agreed, "as long as it's just potato chips and soda, and you tell me how much to get."

Jason yelled hello to me as I walked past his house, but I didn't stop to talk to him with all I had on my mind. I was really in for it tonight, and to follow through on my threat, I had to move my belongings into the nursery, besides.

I blinked when I saw a strange woman sitting on our front steps holding Meredith in her lap.

"Hi," I said. "Who are you?"

The smile she'd been giving the baby slipped away as she looked up at me. Her blue eyes were too close together, and her blond hair was slicked back in a ponytail, but she was youngish, like in her twenties, and almost pretty.

"Are you Case or Jen?" she asked me.

"Case. You're not the new baby-sitter *already*?" I couldn't believe the parents could have found anyone so fast. I'd only just made the suggestion.

"I'm Charlene. The agency sent me. Your father hired me this morning, and I've been with the baby all day. He said to tell you he was looking at some office space."

"Great." I sat down beside her on the step, pleased that she was young like I'd hoped. I was eager to get to know her. "Merry looks happy," I said. "Did she yell your ear off?"

"Why should she? Your father told me she cries a lot. Well, she won't anymore, not with me. Will you,

43

angel girl?" Her voice went from flat to fluty when she spoke to Meredith.

Meredith gave a happy squeal, and I chuckled in surprise. "Do you live near here?" I asked.

"Not that near."

I looked at the curb, and realizing that the beat-up blue pickup parked there might be hers, I asked her about it.

"I borrowed it," she said.

"I always thought it would be fun to ride in the back of a pickup—on a nice day, anyway," I said to make conversation.

"Your mother told me I don't have to do anything for you or your sister. I'm just supposed to take care of the baby," Charlene said, as if she thought I was asking her for something.

"Well, sure. We can take care of ourselves. Jen's fifteen and I'm twelve. I mean—we can probably help *you* out."

"I don't need any help." She wasn't smiling at all now.

Somehow I seemed to be rubbing her the wrong way. "You met my mother today?" I asked, hoping that was a neutral question.

"She came during her lunch hour. She says I won't be seeing her much. She leaves for work before I come and gets home real late. Is she a career woman?"

"Yes, I guess so. I mean, she's got a pretty important job that means a lot to her. She's a manager of finance. Jen, my sister, is good with numbers, too. Me, I'm terrible."

That didn't get any response from Charlene, who was rocking Meredith rhythmically back and forth. I kissed the baby's soft cheek gently and offered, "I can't believe Merry went a whole day without crying. She's never done that before. You must have a magic touch."

"She can tell she's in loving hands," Charlene said confidently.

"She's been in loving hands since she was born, and that hasn't stopped her from yelling," I said.

Ignoring me, Charlene stood up and carried Merry over to the patch of hyacinths. "Smell, angel. Smell the sweet flowers?" Charlene cooed.

I wondered if carrying Meredith around all the time was what was keeping her content. "Have you been a full-time baby-sitter before, Charlene?" I asked.

She turned around and fixed her eyes on me. Then she said, "Your mother already asked me all those questions. Don't you have any chores to do?"

I got the message. She wanted me to go away and stop bothering her, but when I stood up to oblige, I got stuck on an exit line. Finally, I muttered, "Well, I guess I could go start my math homework."

Charlene nodded.

"I guess I'll see you tomorrow, then?"

"Do you always talk so much?" Charlene asked.

"I like to talk. Don't you?"

"No. No. I like to listen. You want to hear things, you have to be still and listen."

She sounded like a teacher, so sure of herself, and she seemed to mean more than what it sounded like on the surface, but I wasn't about to ask her what. "I know what I'll do," I said. "I'll go start moving my stuff into the nursery."

"The nursery? You mean the baby's room? What stuff are you moving in there?"

"Well, I'm switching bedrooms. Actually, the nursery used to be my room. So I'm just moving back in."

"You can't," Charlene said.

"It's okay. I already asked my mother."

She shook her head. Her lips formed words, but she didn't say them. Finally, she got out, "It would be bad for the baby. She needs quiet."

"I won't bother her," I said. "I love my sister. She and I are going to be best buddies as soon as she quiets down."

"No." Charlene was still shaking her head. "You can't be in there."

That got to me. She had charge of my sister, but she didn't have charge of me. "My mother gave me permission," I repeated.

Charlene turned her back on me abruptly. Merry began to whimper. As I walked away, I heard Charlene soothing Meredith, who quieted right away. Charlene might be good with babies, but her personality was pretty negative. I didn't like her much, and obviously, she didn't like me at all.

·FIVE·

The more I thought about Charlene's not wanting me to room with my baby sister, the more indignant I got. Charlene didn't even know me! Meredith would be lucky to have a big sister like me around to pick up dropped rattles and answer important questions.

I reenergized myself with a bowl of Chunky Chocolate ice cream and went up to tackle moving. First I gathered what was on the floor—it was all mine except for Jen's slippers—and dumped the pile on my bed. Then I scooped everything on top of the dresser into a half-empty drawer and used another for what was on the desk. Then I lugged the drawers, one by one, into the nursery. From the nursery window, I caught a glimpse of Charlene handing the baby over to Gerry and going off in her blue truck. I was working on the closet when Jen walked in.

"You're *really* moving in with Meredith?" Jen asked.

"I am," I said, and with a long sigh reminded her, "Now you won't be bothered with my messy presence anymore." She didn't fall on her knees and beg me to stay, but she offered to help with the furniture.

"Won't you miss me a little?" I cued her.

"You'll be right next door, Case." She smiled. "And I'll probably see you at meals."

Sometimes she sounded just like Mother. "You don't care about me anymore," I said. "You really don't. Remember how, when we lived in Stamford, we used to go to the harbor together and talk and talk, and how, when you lived in New York with Mother, she made you use a *timer* on our phone calls because we had so much to say to each other and it was long distance?"

"She never made me use a timer. You're exaggerating, Case."

"Yes, she did. You just don't want to remember that you *used* to tell me everything. I was your best friend when we lived in Stamford."

"Don't be silly. Nothing's changed. You're my sister, and I still love you. But I don't love the way you steal my socks and leave the room looking like a laundry basket. Besides, you talk while I'm trying to do homework."

What could I say? I sighed heavily, but she frowned disapprovingly, and it was a standoff. After that, we each took a side of my dresser and hauled it next door. "Did Dad tell you he found a baby-sitter already, Jen?"

"He says she's a gem," Jen said. "I haven't seen him this happy since the day Meredith was born."

"She may be a gem with Merry, but she's not nice to me. Would you believe she told me I couldn't move into the nursery?"

"Well, having you there'll make her job harder."

"How?" I asked indignantly.

"You know, keeping the room neat and quiet."

"Jen, that's mean. I told you I'm reformed."

We'd returned to Jen's room, and instead of answering me, she stood with her eyebrow up like Mother's, looking at the mountain of mostly purple clothing on my bed. The mountain had outcroppings of schoolbooks and essentials like my Walkman and my heart pillows, plus a few old stuffed animals.

"Come on," I said, ignoring the eyebrow. "Grab an armful and help me." I get tired of being criticized all the time. In silence, we moved the clothes and then the mattress next door.

Gerry came bounding upstairs in time to help with the box spring and the bedframe and my brass headboard.

"It's my lucky day," he exulted as we maneuvered through the doors. "I found a room behind a dress shop with good light, and the rent's reasonable. I can even walk there, which means your mother can stick with her regular car pool schedule. . . . How did you like Charlene, Case?"

The phone rang before I could answer. Jen dropped her corner of the bedframe and rushed downstairs, still hoping Charlie would give in, I guess. "Gerry," she called. "It's for you."

"Mrs. Thompson," Jen whispered to me when she came back up.

I whimpered and thought of hiding in the closet. Instead, Jen helped me put the bed back together, then disappeared into her room, in a hurry to be alone again, no doubt. I considered folding my clothes neatly into drawers to start myself off right but decided I didn't have the time. Gerry wasn't going to be on the phone long with Mrs. Thompson. Quickly, I shoved everything under the bed except for the Walkman, which I was going to need as soon as Merry woke up from her nap downstairs.

Jen appeared with stuff from the top shelf of her closet—my craft materials and my old Barbie doll and more old pillows, quickstitched or appliquéd by me. I hadn't forgotten them. I figured to leave them where they were. "I guess you don't want me to have an excuse to enter your room again," I said.

"Stop trying to make me feel guilty," she said. "I'm just helping you."

Meredith's closet was empty except for a few tiny outfits on hangers and a huge carton of diapers.

"Just dump everything in there," I told Jen. I also shoved in all my bags of fabric, my paints and Magic Markers, plus boxes of pictures and postcards and games. The closet was crammed when we'd finished. We had to stack the books, which had shared space on Jen's bookshelves, against the wall beside my bed.

No sooner did we finish than I got the call of doom from Gerry. "Case, I want to see you."

In a burst of inspiration, I thought of taking a bath. They couldn't attack me while I was lying defenseless in the tub. "I'm in the bathroom," I yelled down to him and, whipping my clothes off, made it into the tub in five seconds.

The water had cooled, and my fingers and toes had puckered from their soaking, when Jen came into the bathroom to tell me Mother was home, and they were waiting for me to come down to dinner.

"How mad? Like boiling or lukewarm?" I asked.

"They're not glad."

I dried myself off and raked through the clothes under my bed to find the cute little nightgown Jen had given me for Christmas. I'd been saving it in case I ever got invited to a sleepover. It was printed with red and blue hearts, and it made me look sweet. If I ever needed to look sweet, it was now. I even brushed my hair.

Meredith's bouncer was on the kitchen counter being pumped by Jen, but Meredith was fussing and squawking, even so. "I'm sorry I didn't come down to help set the table," I said.

"What are you doing in a nightgown this early?" Mother asked. "Oh, never mind. Sit down."

I sat.

"It seems that once again I have to take time off from work to talk to your teacher, Case," Mother began, "and you know how that makes me feel."

I nodded. "But it wasn't my fault. Thompson never listens to me."

"*Mrs.* Thompson. If you'd show her some respect—"

"I do. I'm innocent, Mother. I was defending the student teacher because the boys were giving her a hard time. That's all. Willie will tell you."

"Your teacher says it isn't so much what you do as your attitude, that you go around calling attention to yourself. She says you're arrogant."

"That's mean! What a mean thing to say. Call Willie, Mother. Call Andrea. They'll tell you Mrs.

Thompson picks on me because she hates me."

"Why must you always be so contrary?" Mother asked. "Why can't you get along with adults in authority?"

"I *do* get along. I'm a good kid. Jen!" I called on my sister for help.

"Case means well, Mother," Jen said.

"Meaning well is not enough. She's got to stop behaving so immaturely," Mother said.

"Me? I behave immaturely?"

"What do you call showing off, talking back to teachers, putting your feet on tables? Does that sound mature?"

It was hopeless. "So if you and Thompson already decided that, what do you have to go in to see her for?" I asked.

"There you go," Mother said, "mouthing off just the way your teacher says."

"But I haven't done anything really wrong, and you're treating me like a criminal," I wailed.

"I'm disappointed in you, Case," Mother said, grim-faced. "Your father and I will have to talk this over and decide what to do about it."

"You're going to send me to reform school, right? Just because I tried to help somebody."

"Why must you be so dramatic?" Mother held up her hand. "Don't answer. That's enough now. We'll have dinner and discuss this some other time."

I got in the last word, but it didn't do me any good. I said, "I can't help who I am." But I don't think they believed me.

We ate in silence. I wondered what they'd do to punish me: not reform school maybe, but no TV for a week, no allowance ever again, even no seventh-grade party. Mother continued looking grim while Gerry babbled about how wonderful Charlene was with the baby and how amazing it was that the agency had sent her an hour after he'd called them. Mother's grimness was making my insides crawl.

I felt even worse when Jason's mother called. Gerry answered and put his hand over the receiver to tell Mother. "She wants to know if it's all right to hire Case to baby-sit for Jason Saturday."

"Isn't Jen available?" Mother looked from Gerry to Jen questioningly.

"She says he specifically asked for Case," Gerry said.

"Case is good with Jason," Jen said. "He even told me she's more fun than me. I don't mind, Mother."

"Tell her no," Mother said.

"Why?" I cried.

"If you're too immature to handle yourself, you certainly can't be trusted with a five-year-old boy."

That did it. I slumped in my chair in defeat.

They had ice cream for dessert, but I didn't want any. Meredith stopped chewing on her fists and waving her feet in the air and began yowling. "I'm going to Willie's," I muttered. Nobody said I couldn't; so I got dressed and left.

Willie was cleaning his fish tank.

"Well, I moved into Meredith's room," I told him.

"Is she glad?"

"She doesn't know yet. Tonight's our first night together."

"Good luck."

"My mother's mad at me. Thompson called, and they have to go in to hear about how rotten I am. Mother's so mad she won't even let me baby-sit for Jason, even though he asked for me. Can you believe it, Willie?"

"You'll be done with Thompson in less than a month. Next year you might get a teacher who likes you."

"You don't think I'm a show-off, do you?"

"No."

"Well, what do you think of me?"

He blew out his lips, which made him look like a snub-nosed goldfish, a cute one. "I told you, Case. I think you're okay."

"Well, would you go to the seventh-grade party with me?"

"Sure, if you want to go."

I blinked. I hadn't expected to catch him that easily. "Andrea wants to double-date with us. She got asked."

"Date? We're too young to date."

"Well, do you know how to dance, Willie?"

"No."

"Okay, I'll teach you. Let's go down to your family room and find some good tapes."

"Dancing is not for me," Willie said. "I thought you wanted to go to the party to play games. I'm good at darts."

"We can play games, but we should dance a couple of dances, too."

"Why?"

"Because we're getting older."

"Not me. When I'm old enough to make a fool of myself on the dance floor, I'll let you know."

"Couldn't we just try it?"

"Listen," he said. "I'm not double-dating with Andrea. I'm not dancing with anybody. And I'm not going to the party if that's what you want to go for."

I'd never heard Willie so forceful. I was impressed. "Want me to help you wash the pebbles?"

"No, thanks. I've got it down to a science. Pet Zeus or something till I'm done, and then we can play a game."

Watching how coordinated Willie was at siphoning water and capturing guppies in nets and stuff like that, I figured it couldn't take long to teach him to dance. The party was the weekend after next. Plenty of time to teach him. I picked up a *Natural History* magazine and began looking at the pictures.

Meredith was asleep when I ambled into my new bedroom. The night-light next to her crib lit the room up just enough to see, and the light wouldn't bother me. I'm a good sleeper. I was just dozing off when she began fussing. A few peeps. The crib creaking as she moved. I went over and peered through the bars of her crib, hoping she wouldn't notice me. She looked as if she might have a gas pain. I turned her over on her stomach. She's started rolling over already, but not necessarily when she wants to. She kept lifting her head and arching her body and crying little short spurts. So I tried picking her up and putting her over my shoulder to burp her. Ah, there, a big one.

"That feel better?" I asked her.

She frowned at me as if to say, Who wants to know? If the family thinks I'm difficult, wait until Meredith grows up. She's going to be one tough cookie. I laid her back down, but she continued to fidget, stretching her arms back and throwing her legs up. Any minute she was going to cry again. I felt inside her diaper. Wet, sure enough.

"Okay," I said. "This is the last thing I'm going to do for you. Then I'm going to sleep, and you can scream all you want."

I laid her on the towel on her dresser top and held her in place with one hand while I dipped down to get a clean diaper from the drawer. By the time I had her changed and back in bed again, I was really sleepy.

That did it, I thought with satisfaction, because she was quiet. I rolled into my bed and started a day-dream about winning a dance contest and having long straight hair down to my tiny waist and a partner who told me I was the most beautiful girl in the room. We were doing a slow dance in the dream, and I had half drifted off to sleep when Meredith got going good and strong again. I couldn't remember where I'd stowed my Walkman; so I put my head under the pillow. You know, she came through loud and clear? I waited. Let the parents take care of her. She was their problem, after all.

I kept waiting. I was wide awake, and nobody'd come. Like a good big sister, I got up and went over to the crib. "Hey, you," I said sharply. "What's the matter with you now?"

That got her attention. She looked up at me too startled to scream. I hung my teeth over my lower lips and wrinkled my nose for her. She stared in silent fascination. I pulled my lips wide with my thumbs. She kept staring. Challenged, I made more faces to amuse her. Except I must have made one too many, and she got scared and began screaming louder than ever. Frantically, I went back to faces she'd liked before, but she just kept howling as if she were being murdered, at least.

"Case!" Mother said from the doorway. She was standing there in her red lace nightgown. "What are you doing to that baby? How *could* you when you know how hard it is to get her to sleep?"

"She liked it. I was amusing her."

"I bet." Mother picked Merry up and began burping her.

"I already did that," I said.

"It's probably a bad idea for you to stay in this room. You're better off with Jen."

"See," I cried. "See how you misunderstand me? I was being good."

"Oh, Case," Mother said, and swished out of the room with the baby in her arms. The routine was that Mother would take Meredith into the parental bed and rub her back, or something, until she finally fell asleep. Then she'd be returned to her crib.

I threw myself onto my bed. Why was I always in trouble? Even my own mother didn't trust me. She probably hated me, too, just like Mrs. Thompson. I

57

wondered if I was awful somehow and just couldn't see myself from the outside, the way they saw me. But if I didn't see myself as awful, how was I going to make myself change? It's lucky I'm a good sleeper, or I'd have been awake all night trying to figure that one out.

·SIX·

"So how was your first night with Meredith?" Jen asked me when I plunked my cereal bowl on the table next to her.

"I slept."

Jen shook her head in disbelief.

"I hope you girls cleaned up the bathroom after yourselves," Mother said. Her eyes were on me, not Jen, of course. "Charlene shouldn't have to deal with hair in the sink and wet towels on the floor."

"She only takes care of Meredith?" Jen asked. "No cooking or cleaning or anything?"

"Well," Mother said, "she agreed to start dinner for us if she has the time, and she'll do the baby's wash and feed her. That's enough for what we're paying her."

Meredith was in the bouncer on the kitchen counter watching the lights on the microwave. "I don't think Merry screams as much as she used to," I said. "I think she's growing out of it like the doctor said."

"Your imagination's working overtime again, Case," Mother said. "Listen, Gerry and I'll be late tonight. We've got that appointment with Mrs. Thompson. And Charlene's supposed to leave at five. Jen, can you cover?"

"I'm going to be late, too," Jen said. "Friday's my computer club."

"No problem," I said. "I'll take charge."

Mother eyed me dubiously.

"Case is good with the baby. You can trust her," Gerry put in for me. He'd just come back from toting his drawing board to the car to take to his new office. He looked like his cheerful, old, easygoing self.

"There's my sweet Dad-o." I blew him a kiss.

"If I can trust her, why do I have to leave work early for a special conference with her teacher?" Mother demanded.

"Because Mrs. Thompson's a pill," I said.

"All her fault, huh?" Mother asked. She finished her muffin and took her plate to the dishwasher, telling Gerry, "Be sure you ask Charlene if she wants us to mail those forms I filled out for her to the agency. Oh, and remind her to bring the references if she forgets them today."

"Relax," Gerry said. "Everything'll be fine now. You know all that stuff we read about bonding? You should have seen Charlene bond with Meredith the instant she saw her. It was beautiful."

"How old is this woman?" Jen asked.

"Twenty-eight," Mother said. "She was a little vague about what she's been doing since high school. Apparently she was needed at home to raise her younger siblings. Her mother got ill or something. But if Charlene finished high school at eighteen, that would be ten years of helping out—which is mind-boggling."

"So she's not ambitious," Gerry said. "The important thing is she loves babies."

"And it's nice that she's not an old lady," Jen said.

"I suppose," Mother granted. "And maybe she's just doing this as a temporary thing until she gets settled in this area. She comes from a little town in upstate New York, and she did indicate some other job experiences—cleaning in a motel and waitressing." Mother sounded uneasy. "It was a sort of hurried interview. I had a meeting to get back to."

"Listen, if she can handle Meredith, what more do we need to know?" Gerry said.

"Well, more about her in general," Mother murmured.

"Don't worry," I put in. "I'll find out all about her."

"Don't you pester her with questions, Case," Gerry said.

"Pester her? I thought *you* had faith in me, Dad."

"Just try to be helpful and cooperative," Mother instructed me.

"And remember," Gerry said, "we need her desperately."

"I know. I will. I promise."

A car horn tooted for Mother then, and she rushed out. Gerry went back to the porch to finish packing his art materials. He planned to leave when Charlene arrived.

"I'll do the bathroom," Jen said to me. "You better fix up the nursery."

"I haven't been in it long enough to mess it up," I said, but I went back upstairs and made my bed. I even put the purple-flowered bedspread on. I hadn't used it in so long that I'd forgotten how pretty it was. I didn't have time, before I raced up the hill to the school bus, to do anything about the stuff under the bed, but the bedspread hid it pretty well. Gerry was jouncing Meredith when I got downstairs.

"You better stick up for me with Mrs. Thompson this afternoon," I told him, "or you won't be my favorite father anymore."

"You better get along with Charlene, or you won't be my favorite, either," he said.

Tippy was in the girls' room, making up a student to be an old bag lady for a play. "Mrs. Thompson called my parents, and they're coming in to see her today," I told Tippy as I washed my hands.

"Don't blame me, Case," she said. "I tried to tell her that you were defending me yesterday, but she wouldn't listen."

Tippy was brushing gray powder under the bag lady's eyes. I watched the girl age fifty years as Tippy shaded her nose and drew lines on her forehead. "You're really good at doing makeup," I said.

"I learned it in drama school. I was going to be an actress, until my mother talked me into becoming a teacher."

Another dissatisfied mother, I thought. "My mother would like to talk me into becoming something else, too. She's not too thrilled with me," I confided. "Well, she hasn't sentenced me yet."

"I hope you get off easy," Tippy said.

I hung around until the bag lady had left and Tippy was putting her makeup kit away, because I had an idea. "Tippy, would you do me a big favor and call my mother and tell her you think I'm a good kid? She might believe Thompson has it in for me if you told her."

"Oh, I don't know, Case." Tippy bit her plump lower lip. "Mrs. Thompson might not like that. It's kind of like going over her head, if you know what I mean."

"But it's the truth, isn't it?"

"But see, I can't afford to get Mrs. Thompson mad at me. She writes my recommendation. You understand, don't you?"

I understood that, cute and friendly as Tippy was, she was a coward, or else she didn't like me enough to stick her neck out for me. Whichever, it was too bad.

Mr. Sobel, our biology teacher, was passing out test papers when I walked into his room. He handed me mine without asking where I'd been. Something about the look he gave me made me check my grade. "Wow!" I said. I had a 96.

Sobel grinned at me. "You got the highest mark in the class."

I collapsed into my seat next to Willie. Usually he gets the highest grade in science, but he'd skipped the last question because he'd run out of time from writing margin notes about how the answer could be different depending on how you interpreted it. Simple questions can get complicated when Willie answers them.

I could tell by the quirk in his lip when I flashed my mark at him that he was pleased for me.

It was raining when I got home, a nice, warm, misty rain. I came in the kitchen door and nearly stepped on Meredith, who was lying belly down on the vinyl floor. "Whoops! What are you doing there, munchkin?" I asked.

"She's practicing rolling," Charlene said. She was sitting at the kitchen table, drinking a cup of something steaming.

"So you're becoming a roller, Merry mite. How about that?" I picked her up, and she fixed me with her blue eyes, mouth open and lips moving as if she'd like to say something. "You ready to travel?" I asked her. "Thinking of rolling right out the door?"

"Babies need to move around. They don't like to be confined all the time," Charlene said.

"Really?" The teacher tone made me ask, "Did you learn that in school?"

"School doesn't teach you about babies," Charlene said.

"So where did you learn, then?"

"I've been taking care of babies since I was seven years old. I love babies."

"Me, too," I said. "I'm planning on having a big family."

Her close-together, blue eyes narrowed in on me.

"Is that so? You're not going to have a career like your mama?"

"Well," I said, "I guess I'll do that, too."

She snorted scornfully.

"You don't think you can have a career and raise a big family, besides?" I asked.

"Babies need you to be there for them with your whole heart all the time." Merry began to squawk. "Give her here," Charlene ordered.

Curious to see how Charlene would quiet her, I handed Merry over. What Charlene did wasn't much different from what we did. She put Merry over her shoulder and patted her back, and when that didn't work, she laid Merry over her knees and rubbed her tummy. That made Merry relax. "I guess you do have a magic touch," I said.

Charlene smiled. "It's not magic," she said. "This baby knows me. She knew the minute we met that I was hers."

I wondered if that was possible, that a baby could sense things about people. Mother would never believe it. She'd think Charlene was strange. Something about her was a little off, but I couldn't put my finger on what exactly. Except that she wasn't wearing any jewelry, not even a ring, she looked like any regular young woman in her clean faded jeans and print blouse with her blond hair tied back neatly from her face.

I got out the milk and a glass and settled down at the table. Meanwhile Charlene was laying Meredith down on the kitchen floor. "You don't worry about germs?" I asked.

"What germs?"

"I mean, the floor," I said. "I guess it's clean, but we walk on it so—"

"This baby won't get sick from anything *I* do with her," Charlene said.

"Well, but I took a special child care course and learned about sterilizing things a baby might stick in its mouth."

"They teach you all kinds of stuff. That doesn't make it true." Charlene spoke as if she had superior knowledge.

"You know," I said, to see what she'd tell me, "I don't understand why Meredith's been screaming her head off with us. Why doesn't she know that we all love her, too?"

"Because you aren't there for her. You go to school, and her mama and papa work, and none of you are altogether hers." Suddenly, as if she were overcome with emotion, she scooped Merry up and cuddled her under her chin. I shivered. Seeing them like that, it seemed that Merry belonged to Charlene. They even looked alike, both blond and blue-eyed like Gerry. Mother and I have dark hair and eyes, and Jen's coloring's in-between.

"Are there any cookies left?" I asked, getting up to check the cookie jar.

"I don't eat sweets," Charlene said. She lowered Meredith to her lap. The baby lay quietly gazing up into her eyes.

"Watching your figure?" I asked, and took out a couple of Fig Newtons.

"No." I bit into a cookie and she added, "Sugar's

bad for you, like alcohol. It makes you crazy."

"Umm," I joked, "maybe *that's* what's wrong with Gerry and me. We're the sweet eaters in this family."

"Glah," Merry said, kicking her legs. "Glah, gah, gah."

"Don't you have any friends to visit?" Charlene asked abruptly.

"You mean you want to get rid of me again?" I was being funny, but she answered me without a trace of humor.

"I don't like talking. I told you yesterday. Being quiet's best—it brings you peace." She looked upset, although I couldn't imagine how I'd upset her.

"Charlene, I'm just trying to get to know you," I explained. "I'm the one who'll be around most when you're here; so I want us to be friends."

Charlene looked at me blankly. Then she stood up. "I'm taking Baby to her room. You stay down here." Her voice sharpened. "And tomorrow you better clear out all that stuff you shoved under the bed. You better clean up after yourself if you want to stay in her room."

As soon as Mother and Gerry came through the door, Mother asked me, "How was she?"

"Weird," I said. "She thinks it's good for the baby to roll around the kitchen floor. She thinks Merry knew her when they met. She thinks she knows *everything* about babies, and she's so emotional."

"Look who's talking," Mother said.

"Mother, will you listen to me? Charlene believes babies can feel how much you love them."

"Well . . ." Mother surprised me by hesitating and then saying thoughtfully, "Who knows?"

"But putting a baby on the floor—that's not hygienic," I sputtered in desperation.

Mother shrugged and said, "The floor's probably clean enough so long as she doesn't lick it."

"Mother!" I protested.

Gerry had gone upstairs to check on Meredith. Now he returned to announce, "She's sound asleep and looking beautiful."

"Dinner's not started, I see," Mother said. She sighed. "I guess you can't have everything."

I waited for them to tell me about the meeting with Mrs. Thompson, but Gerry went to the living room to watch the six o'clock news.

Unable to bear the suspense, I asked Mother, who was rummaging through the refrigerator in search of leftovers, "Did Thompson fill your ears with awful stuff about me?"

"Gerry defended you," Mother said. She pulled the salad drawer out and carried it over to the sink.

I began setting the table. "Not you, though," I muttered. Mother wanted to know what I'd said. "Nothing. Anyway, it can't have been too bad because I haven't done anything too bad."

"Mrs. Thompson's worried that you're heading for trouble. She says you haven't learned to get along in a group, that you're always setting yourself up to be noticed in a negative fashion."

"I just stand up for what I think is right, Mother."

Mother sighed. "Let's hope you grow out of it. Look at how Jen's changed since she discovered boys.

She used to be so quiet and shy, and now she's practically cheerleader material."

"You want *me* to become a cheerleader?" I was horrified.

"Why not?" Mother grinned. "It'd make you easier to live with."

"So would a frontal lobotomy."

"Case!"

"Well, that's what you're saying, that you can't stand me the way I am, that I'm a horrible person. But I don't *feel* horrible, even though you're trying to make me." I stormed upstairs to my room, passing Jen, who was just getting home.

"What's the matter?" she asked.

"Do you want me to change my personality, Jen?"

"How?"

"So I don't stick out. So I'm just like everybody else."

"No," Jen said, and she put her arm around me comfortingly. "You get knocked down a lot because you stick out, but at least you do stick out. I don't, and that's what makes me such a boring person."

I'll never understand why Jen has this thing about not liking herself. "Oh, come on," I said. "You're not ordinary. You're my super sister." I hugged her, grateful that she, at least, still approved of me.

It was raining so hard that I ran all the way across the yards to Willie's house. Andrea had asked me today if I'd taught Willie to dance yet. He hadn't even agreed to let me.

"You're all wet," Willie said when he opened the

door. He was watching a TV program about animals. I sat down beside him on the fat plaid cushions of the couch in the family room. He could talk to me because the commercials were on.

"Were your parents happy about your mark?" he asked.

"What mark? Oh, that. I forgot to tell them."

"You're upset, huh? They give you a hard time after seeing Thompson?"

"No," I said, "they didn't even say much . . . yet."

"Well, what's wrong, then?"

All at once everything that was wrong in my life lumped in my chest, and I sniffled a little instead of answering him. I think it was my sniffles that did it, because after the program, Willie let me start to teach him how to dance.

Did you ever see anyone seize up with fear at the sound of dance music? Willie went rigid, positively rigid.

"Just sway," I said, realizing I'd have to start with basics. "Just stand there and *feel* the rhythm with your body. Relax, let the music move *you*."

Half an hour later I gave up, for the evening, anyway. Willie's idea of feeling the rhythm was to bend his knees slightly and pump up and down with his arms dangling stiffly. He looked like an oil well rig.

Finally, I danced around by myself to show him how easy it was. He said, "You're a good dancer, Case. You're really light on your feet."

"Thanks. I love dancing."

"It's too bad," he said sadly.

"Why?"

"'Cause I don't."

I told him about Charlene then. Willie's opinion was it didn't matter whether she was strange or not so long as she was good with the baby.

"Maybe," I said. "I'm going to keep an eye on her, though, because I'm the only one who'll be around her much—if she lets me be. I don't think she likes me."

"Maybe she just needs to get used to you," he said.

"You mean I take getting used to?"

"Well, you're different, Case."

"Yeah? So are you."

"Uh-huh, that's why we're friends," he said calmly.

"You were right about Tippy," I said, thinking about how she'd refused to support me with my parents. "She doesn't care about us."

"You mean we can forget the party?"

"No. It'll be fun." I remembered I still had to finish the hearts that spelled out WE LOVE YOU. Also, I had to take all my belongings from under my bed and stow them neatly in drawers to please Charlene. Well, tomorrow was Saturday. I had time.

"Don't worry, Willie. Everything'll work out." I patted his back. "And the next dancing lesson will be better. You'll see."

He groaned. "I should have known you'd never give up on anything."

I went home feeling fine. After all, the conference with Mrs. Thompson was past, and nothing had happened to me. Also, Charlene might not be as strange as I thought. What was so bad about loving babies, anyway? Maybe I was imagining things. Maybe we were lucky to have her. Well, time would tell.

·SEVEN·

I was so good Saturday, I could hardly believe it myself. It took me most of the afternoon to box or hang everything I owned in the closet or fold it neatly away in a dresser drawer. But when I went downstairs to get applause for what I'd done, I ran head on into trouble.

"Case," Mother said, before I opened my mouth, "how would you like to spend the summer at camp?"

"Huh? Why should I go to camp? I'm spending the summer with Jen at the pool. Besides, I can't go away. Willie would be lonely without me. And Meredith would miss me. And Jen and Gerry." I left an opening for Mother to say she'd miss me, too. Naturally, she ignored it.

"This is a special skills camp," she explained. "Your father and I think it would do you good."

"What do you mean, special skills?"

"Interpersonal relationships. It sounds like fun. You put up your own shelter with your group, and cook your meals, and each group plans its own activities."

"What is this?" I asked suspiciously. "A working reform school? A camp for misfits?"

"It's expensive," Mother said, waving aside my questions. "But your father and I feel that we sent Jen to computer camp last year, and now it's your turn."

"I don't want to go to computer camp, and I certainly don't want to go to a summer reform school. Is this my punishment from your talk with Mrs. Thompson?"

"Case!" Mother said. "This isn't a punishment. It's to help you."

"Like not being allowed to sit for Jason?"

"That was a punishment," Mother admitted.

The telephone rang. It was Andrea. I didn't know she had my telephone number. "Hi," she said. "I called to find out what they did to you."

"What who did to me?"

"Your parents after Mrs. Thompson talked to them."

"They want to send me to summer camp."

"Really? Boy, you're lucky. My father would have yelled so loud you'd hear him clear across town, and that'd be just for starters."

"My parents don't yell," I said glumly. "Only my baby sister yells, and even she doesn't much anymore." It occurred to me again that she probably was growing out of it, with or without Charlene's magic touch.

"Well, you're lucky," Andrea repeated. "So how are the dance lessons coming?"

"We only had one so far."

"And?"

"I think he's hopeless, Andrea."

"Oh, Case. You have to get him to dance. You have to."

"Why? We can go to the party with you and watch. Your mother will never know."

"It wouldn't be any fun for you that way."

"It wouldn't be any fun for Willie any other way."

When I got off the phone, Mother was doing bills at the desk. "No camp," I told her. "You can think of some other way to punish me. I'm not going."

"Cool it," Mother said. "Would you go out front and see if you can help your father with Meredith? She's screaming."

I could hear her.

Gerry had taken her for a walk around the neighborhood in a stroller. "She doesn't like lawn mowers," he said gloomily when I went outside and asked what Meredith was upset about. "Or dogs or the wind or anything. Maybe we ought to hire Charlene to take care of her weekends, too." He sounded discouraged, but I was too angry to sympathize.

"How could you agree to let Mother send me off to a reform school camp?" I demanded.

"It's supposed to be a good place. But I didn't think you'd want to go."

"Well, I don't and you can't make me."

"Don't worry. We won't try . . . unless we hear from your school again."

Being good had better become a permanent condition, I realized, at least until school was over.

75

"Rats," I said out loud, "rats, vermin and venomous toads."

The rusty pickup truck was parked in front of our house when I got home from school Monday afternoon, but I could hear Meredith crying. Charlene's magic mustn't be working. I came in through the kitchen door and found them on the living room rug. The baby was naked, and Charlene was stroking her stomach with a soft-bristled brush. "It doesn't sound as if she likes being tickled," I said.

Charlene jumped. She hadn't heard me come in. "She liked it. You should have heard her laughing."

"Uh-huh," I said. "But maybe Merry's had enough. I read somewhere that tickling's a form of torture."

Charlene stopped tickling. "*I* know what she likes," she said, and picked the baby up, turning her back on me as she rocked Meredith, who stopped crying.

"So how'd your day go?" I was already used to talking to Charlene's back.

"We went to the park. Didn't we, Baby?" Charlene's voice went high and sweet when she directed it to Meredith. "You got lots of fresh air and sunshine today, didn't you?"

"That's nice," I said. "Did she yell all the way?" I was remembering Meredith's reaction to the infant car seat, or maybe just to being in the car, when Mother and Jen and I had gone to the shopping mall yesterday.

"Why would she? She knows she's safe with me," Charlene boasted.

"She's safe with us, too, but you should have heard her in the car yesterday."

"I carry her right against my heart."

"Not in the car seat?" I asked in alarm. "I think that's against the law."

"A baby needs to feel her mother's heartbeat," Charlene informed me.

"But you're not her mother, Charlene."

Meredith began sounding unhappy again. Charlene stood up and marched off to the kitchen with her. I followed in time to see Charlene take a green plastic box with a snap-buttoned lid from a big purse on the counter. Next, with her back to me and Meredith draped over her shoulder, she got a bottle of brownish stuff from the refrigerator.

She was having a hard time balancing the baby while she opened the bottle . . . so I offered, "I'll hold her for you."

Charlene shot me one of her narrow-eyed looks, but let me take Meredith.

"Hi ya, punkin pot," I said, touching the spongy baby nose with my finger. She opened her mouth for my finger. "Not fussy what you suck on, are you?" I asked her as she swung her head around to catch me. I let her have my knuckle, which was cleaner to suck on, but she mustn't have liked the taste because she pulled back and began to cry.

"You can wait in the living room. I'll bring something to soothe her in a minute," Charlene said.

I got a glimpse of a whole bunch of narrow little bottles filled with tiny pills in the green plastic kit as I turned away. What was Charlene doing? The doctor hadn't prescribed any medicine for Meredith, as far as I knew. It made me nervous to think that Charlene might be giving my little sister something she wasn't supposed to get.

To quiet Meredith, I tried laying her down on the living room rug, as Charlene would, but that didn't help. Meredith was red with temper by the time Charlene showed up with the half-pint bottle of brownish liquid and a little cap with a couple of tiny tablets in it. "What's that?" I asked.

"It's soothing," Charlene said, and popped the tablets into the baby's mouth, following them with the nipple.

Meredith pulled away from the nipple until she'd tasted a drop, then she began sucking busily. "Babies know what's good for them," Charlene said.

"But what'd you give her, and what's in that bottle?"

"Nothing that can hurt her. Just some chamomilla. They've been using it for cranky babies for hundreds of years."

Who's they, I wondered, but I wasn't about to risk getting Charlene mad at me by shoving too many questions at her again. Let my parents deal with her after I told them about it tonight. Setting aside that worry, I tried for a less touchy subject. "How come you have a truck instead of a car, Charlene?"

"It's not my truck. It's Ina's. Tomorrow I'll start coming by bus."

"Oh. Will it be a long trip for you?"

"I don't mind buses."

She was looking at Meredith and not at me. I chatted on. "I haven't tried the buses yet. We've only lived in Livingston since last summer, and I haven't really explored it much. Do you like the town you live in?"

"It's just a place to stay. I don't care about it."

I looked at my watch. Five was when she was supposed to leave, and it was nearly that now. "Listen, Charlene," I said. "Gerry's doing the food shopping on his way home, but you don't have to wait for him. I'll take care of Merry till he gets here."

"You call your father by his first name, but not your mother?"

"Because I knew him as Gerry before he married my mother. He's my stepfather."

"Stepfather?" Charlene looked surprised.

"My father died when I was little," I explained. "Gerry's the only father I've ever known, and actually, I'm closer to him than to my mother."

"I was close to my stepfather, too."

Her voice was so heavy that I asked, "Did something happen to him?"

She didn't answer me. I could feel the shield going up to fend me off. Oh, she was a strange one! And I didn't care how much she loved babies, leaving my sister in her hands made me nervous.

Meredith was finished with her bottle, and I was in the mood for a cuddle. I held out my arms. "Can I have her now?"

Charlene pulled back. The sudden movement

made Merry squeal. Charlene changed her mind then and handed Merry over. She mewed like an anxious kitten in the crook of my arm.

"See," Charlene said with a sly smile, "she can tell how you feel."

"What do you mean, how I feel?" I was so surprised that I let Charlene take the baby back, and Meredith quieted down.

"You know who loves you, don't you, sweet pie?" Charlene cooed at the baby.

"What do you mean?" I repeated indignantly. "I love Merry. I couldn't wait for her to be born."

"Oh, *sure* you love her. What do you care that you're not his favorite anymore, now he's got a real daughter."

Her meanness took my breath away. Finally I protested, "But I'm not jealous of Merry. I couldn't be. She's just a helpless little baby, and anyway, with all the screaming she's been doing, she's not much competition in the Miss Lovable contest."

"Most sisters get jealous when a new one comes along," Charlene said.

"Did you get jealous, Charlene? Is that how you know?"

She whipped around so that her back was toward me again. "I wasn't *ever* jealous of a baby," she said with passion. "Babies come pure from God's hands. I love them more than my own self."

The way she'd said "pure from God's hands" made me wonder if she was a religious fanatic. And what about her stepfather? She'd sounded strange

80

about him, too. Cautiously, I probed, "Was your step-father good to you, Charlene?"

She turned and glared at me. "You shut up now. Just you shut yourself up. You don't know *anything*." Her close-together eyes burned with anger. The sudden rage made my skin crawl. I wondered if I somehow brought out the crazy in her, or if she acted strange with other people, too. I wished Jen would get home from school on time, for a change, so that she could meet Charlene. Of course, Jen wasn't much of a talker. I'd have to get them started if Jen was going to get to know her.

"I didn't mean to make you mad, Charlene," I said. It was true without being an apology.

She calmed down instantly and said, as if she were explaining her anger away, "You just ask too many questions. You bug me, asking so many questions." Then she flashed me a sly look and added, "If I were you, instead of wasting time here, I'd go upstairs and try to get that paint out of the rug."

"What paint?"

"Near your dresser. I saw it when I went in the nursery this morning."

"But I didn't knock anything over."

"You must have done it when you painted all that junk hanging up there," Charlene said. "Go on up and look if you don't believe me."

I figured she was just trying to get rid of me, but I went to look, anyway. I'd finally painted the hearts sign for Tippy's party yesterday and strung it up in the nursery to dry. But I hadn't cleaned up before I went off to the mall with Jen and Mother. Maybe I had knocked a jar over. I'd been in a hurry to go because I'd kind of hoped Mother would buy me a new outfit for the seventh-grade party. She hadn't. When I'd hinted, she'd said she didn't think my school behavior deserved a reward.

My hearts were where I'd left them, pinned to a ribbon and strung from the closet to the curtain rod. Paintbrushes were still soaking in a glass on my dresser, next to the poster paint jars, but below on the rug was a saucer-sized red splotch. I groaned. Mother would kill me when she saw that bloody-looking mess on the new lemon yellow carpet. But how had I done it? Unless it had happened while I was pulling underwear out this morning . . . . My top drawer sticks sometimes, and if I'd jiggled it. . . . But I'd have noticed a jar falling off. *Had* I done it? Maybe it hadn't been me.

Suppose Charlene had knocked over the jar by accident and was using me to cover up? She could even have done it on purpose to get me in trouble so that Mother would kick me out of the nursery. The only trouble was, nobody was likely to believe either idea.

So far, Charlene was in golden with my family just because she had taken Meredith off their hands. They didn't see enough of Charlene to learn anything about her. Gerry stayed home until she came in the morning and was probably in such a rush to get to his drawing board that he'd say, "Hello, nice day, need anything? Good-bye," and take off. Mother went to work before Charlene arrived and returned after she'd left. Jen would have to be the one to back me up when I advised the parents that they'd hired a weirdo. That is, Jen would back me up if I could get her to see what I saw.

I scrubbed at the paint spill with the soap and water that *should* clean up poster paints, but the stain had been there too long. I got it to turn pink and no lighter. What if I *had* spilled the paint without noticing! It wouldn't have hurt Charlene to have tried washing it out, even if it wasn't part of her duties. Unless she hoped it would get me in trouble. How badly did she want me out of the nursery, anyway? I was keeping the room neat. I'd put everything away except the poster paints and the sign.

The sound of voices came to me. Jen was downstairs with Charlene. Great! I hurried to join them.

"Did you taste the cauliflower soup Charlene brought us for dinner?" Jen asked me. She had a spoon and a big plastic container in her hands. "It's good."

"I didn't know about it," I said, puzzled because Jen hated cauliflower. I tasted the soup. It was bland and pasty. Jen was just being polite.

"I made it last night," Charlene said with pride. She took the container and poured its contents into one of our largest pots. "You can have it for dinner. I guess your mother doesn't make homemade soup."

"She doesn't have the time," Jen said. "Anyway, Gerry's the cook in our family. Chicken soup's his specialty."

"Cauliflower's better for you," Charlene said. "They pump chickens full of chemicals, and it's cruel how they raise them, all jammed in together so they can't barely move."

I wrinkled my nose. I'd been feeling guilty about eating chicken ever since I'd learned about how they were grown. "So you're a vegetarian?" I asked.

Charlene nodded. "A vegetarian, and I only eat organically grown food. I buy everything I eat in a natural foods store." The container she was now washing out in the sink was labeled NATURE'S OWN PEANUT BUTTER, NO ADDITIVES OR PRESERVATIVES. I wondered if Charlene bought her peanut butter by the half gallon. I love the stuff, but even I don't eat a half gallon in a year—I don't think.

Jen was eating yogurt. Meredith was on the floor under the table. She seemed pretty happy there with all the chair legs to look at, but I asked, "Why's the baby under the table?"

"So that you don't step on her," Charlene said.

Jen laughed. I guess she thought Charlene was joking. I sat down beside Jen, determined to keep my mouth shut and just listen.

"How did you make out with Mrs. Thompson today?" Jen asked me.

"Fine," I said, not wanting to talk about it in front of Charlene.

"Who's Mrs. Thompson?" Charlene asked.

"Case's homeroom and English teacher," Jen said. "She and Case don't get along."

"Thanks a lot," I said to my sister, "but it so happens I get along fine with her. She just can't get along with me."

84

"I bet you bother her with questions." Charlene said it teasingly, but Jen wasn't about to let anybody else criticize me.

"Case's curious because she's bright," Jen said. "She's the lively one in our family."

"You're quiet, like me," Charlene said to Jen, making it a compliment.

"Merry's going to be the liveliest kid in our family," I said.

Charlene focused her close-together eyes on me and said coldly, "She's going to be a *good* girl." As if she thought I wasn't!

But Jen didn't seem to notice the unspoken jab at me. Still in her Miss Politeness voice she said to Charlene, "It's amazing how well-behaved Meredith is with you."

Charlene just smiled—no mention of the soothing pills, of course. She retrieved Meredith from under the table. I bet carrying Meredith around all day was part of Charlene's magic.

"This baby's going to be talking early," Charlene said. "Watch how she tries to imitate me. Ma," Charlene said to Meredith. "Ma-ma."

"Glah," Meredith said, gleefully waving her hands.

Jen's never found babies too fascinating. She stood up and said, "I guess I'll go up and start my homework. See you tomorrow, Charlene."

Before I could think of an excuse to keep Jen there, she took off.

I followed her upstairs to her bedroom and asked

what she thought of Charlene.

"She seems okay." Jen was laying her schoolbooks out on her desk.

"She tried to tell me I'm jealous because Meredith's Gerry's real daughter," I said.

"Well, so what? You know you're not."

"I *could* be a little jealous," I admitted. "Just sometimes. Just a little when he gets all starry-eyed about Merry and doesn't notice me."

"Don't worry about it, Case. That's natural. I was jealous of you when you were born."

"You were?"

"Sure I was."

"What did you do about it?"

"Nothing much, just ignored you for as long as I could."

That was a revelation. Charlene had been right, then. Were her ideas as weird as I thought? Mother accused me of being dramatic and exaggerating things. Maybe I was exaggerating again. I *could* have spilled the paint without noticing. Maybe. And maybe there was nothing dangerous in that plastic medicine kit or the brown liquid in the baby's bottle. What about taking a baby in a car without a car seat? No problem to that, either, now that Charlene would be coming by bus. It was getting really confusing. Charlene was so sure of everything. Me, I was getting less and less sure.

·EIGHT·

I squatted beside the paint stain, brooding. One look at it and Mother would say, "That does it." Next stop for me would be summer camp reform school where I'd do hard labor with other nonconforming kids. Running away from home wouldn't help, either. Grams was the only one I could run to and she'd send me right back.

The other ideas I came up with weren't much better. For instance, I could cut myself with something sharp, like scissors, and claim that's how the bloody spot got there. That would turn Mother's anger to sympathy fast, but a cut big enough to bleed a lot would hurt too much. I could say that I suspected Charlene had made the spot by accident and wouldn't admit it because she was afraid of losing her job. That might even be true, except I'd hate myself for tattling.

I was prodding my brain for a better idea when Jen came into my room to ask if she could borrow a red pen.

"All I have's a red felt tip," I said without looking up.

"What are you looking for?"

"I'm not looking for. I'm looking at," I said glumly.

She peered over my shoulder. "Oh, Case! Mother's going to kill you."

"No. Just send me to reform school where they'll brainwash me into being just like everybody else. . . . Do you think laundry bleach would work?"

"We could *try* bleach," Jen said. "You stay put. I'll get it." She hurried off.

I stood and stretched, cheered to have her on my side. She came back with the bleach and told me Gerry was home. "Charlene's gone. Gerry's taking the baby out to show her the robin's nest in the backyard."

"Charlene must've convinced him babies understand more than we think," I said, and began tipping the bottle over the spot.

"No, no!" Jen said. "Don't pour that stuff right on. Wet a cloth with it and use that."

"Too late."

We ran for rags and took turns scrubbing at the foamy mess. The red came off just fine, but so did the yellow. Now the new yellow wall-to-wall carpeting had a big white spot right where you could see it from the doorway.

"I could tell Mother I did it," Jen offered. "I'm not in any trouble; so she wouldn't be as mad at me."

"No, thanks." But I gave her a grateful hug for making the offer. We stood side by side staring at the spot. "We could make a polka dot rug by bleaching a few more places," I suggested, not too seriously. "Or we could move the dresser to hide it."

"Mother's going to find it eventually, Case," Jen said.

"Eventually I won't be in trouble with Mrs. Thompson anymore."

"Umm." Jen helped me move the dresser. It stuck out from the wall too much and overlapped the molding around the closet, but it hid the spot. Sort of.

"Jen," I said. "Charlene really is a weirdo. Really." I told her about the bottle of brown stuff and the pills.

"You better let the parents know," Jen said. "What if Charlene's drugging the baby to keep her quiet? They'd get rid of her no matter how much they need her if she's doing that."

We started dinner with the cauliflower soup. Everybody tasted it except Jen. Mother and I had about three spoons each. Gerry got halfway through his bowl before he stopped.

"It's sort of bland and pasty, isn't it?" he said. "But it was nice of her to try. I'll thank her for all of us."

"Thank her and encourage her to cook what's in our refrigerator," Mother said.

"She's a vegetarian," Jen said. "She probably won't know what to do with what's in our refrigerator."

"She could make us a salad," Mother suggested.

I waited patiently until Gerry had finished telling about how he got this funny idea about a runaway lawn mower and was able to finish the whole strip in a day, working without interruption. Then I let Mom tell her news about how she was going to be acting for her boss while he went off to take some course.

"I thought you said your boss didn't trust women managers," Gerry said.

"Apparently he's decided this particular one's as dedicated to getting the job done as he is," Mother answered smugly.

"Well, congratulations to our future senior executive!" Gerry said.

Mother beamed until I asked, "Does this mean you won't get home till midnight now?"

"No, Case, and should I need to put in a few extra hours, it'd only be for the three months that he's gone, anyway."

"In three months Meredith could be dead," I announced.

"What?" both parents yelled at once.

I'd gotten their attention.

The most damning evidence was the pills. I asked, "Did the doctor prescribe a medicine for Meredith called chamomilla?"

"No," Mother said. "What's chamomilla?"

"It's what Charlene gave Merry today."

I began describing the green plastic kit with all the little bottles, but Gerry interrupted to ask Mother, "Isn't chamomile some kind of tea?"

"Yes, flowers or something," Mother said. "It's probably harmless enough, but I'll speak to Charlene. We certainly don't want her dosing our baby with anything the doctor hasn't recommended. I'll call her from work tomorrow."

"You don't have to. I'll talk to her about it in person," Gerry said.

I threw in my next item. "And she's giving Merry some kind of brownish stuff instead of her formula."

"Brownish stuff?" Mother said. "Oh, that's all right, Case. The doctor recommended a new formula for Meredith in case she's lactose intolerant."

I tried item three. "And Charlene carries Merry around all day—when she isn't letting her roll around the floor. Even when she drives her to the park, she doesn't use the car seat; she holds her against her heart." I demonstrated with an imaginary baby.

"What? I can't believe she'd drive holding a baby in her arms," Mother said.

"It'd be awkward," Gerry said, "unless she uses one of those baby slings that you wear around your neck."

"Gerry! Meredith has to be in the car seat for safety's sake," Mother said.

"Right, right. Well, no sweat. I'll just tell Charlene that."

"Don't you *care* that she's weird?" I burst out in frustration. "She thinks babies come pure from God."

"Well," Gerry said, "they do, sort of."

"Being religious doesn't make Charlene weird, Case," Mother said.

I made one last attempt. "And she tried to tell me I'm jealous of the baby."

"So? Lots of kids would be, and it's lovely that you're not. I'm sure she'll appreciate that eventually." Mother's tone was soothing, as if she was trying to calm me down.

"I'm telling you you hired a kook," I insisted.

"Well, she's certainly out of bounds if she's giving

Meredith anything the doctor hasn't recommended."

"Don't worry, ladies," Gerry said. "I'll make sure she gets the message loud and clear."

When they got around to asking me how my day had gone, I couldn't even remember. All I could think of was how Mother was going to react when she saw the bleach spot. I'd be in a whole lot more trouble than I'd managed to get Charlene into. A sneaky little doubt entered my mind. What if the real problem was that Charlene didn't like me, which made her act sly and nasty with me, but otherwise, she was normal? Certainly my parents hadn't been too alarmed by what I'd told them about her. Maybe I was the weird one.

"Case!" Mother yelled when I was watching TV an hour later. "Come up here."

"Da-da-dum," I said to mark my doom.

Jen trotted upstairs after me. "The bleach idea was mine," she said immediately, when we saw Mother staring down at the blotched carpet with her hands on her hips. "Case spilled the paint and she couldn't get it out well enough, so I said—"

"The brand-new carpet!" Mother said. She had shoved the dresser back where it belonged. "Oh, Case. Why couldn't you have painted in the kitchen?"

"Then I would have been in everybody's way," was all I could think of to explain myself.

To my surprise, that was it. I mean Mother moaned and groaned and complained some more about her lovely lemon yellow carpet, but she didn't sentence me to life imprisonment in a camp for misfits, or cancel all TV privileges until I was twenty, or anything. I figured I had Jen to thank for that.

No truck was parked outside when I got home from school the next afternoon. I heard Meredith whimpering on the porch and headed that way.

She was in her bouncer for a change. Charlene was in the bathroom, judging by the sounds I heard from there. "Hi, tweetie," I said to Meredith. Her eyes looked glazed. Her cheeks were flushed, and her forehead felt warm when I kissed it.

"She seems sick," I told Charlene, who appeared behind me.

"No, she's just out of sorts."

"Well, if she has a fever, we should call the doctor, Charlene."

"She's not sick, and, anyway, I already called Ina, and she told me what to do."

"Is Ina a doctor?"

"No. She's a healer, and she knows all about herbs and natural remedies. Doctors don't know anything but drugs and how to charge too much."

"You don't believe in doctors?"

"Not for babies. Doctors act like they know so much, but half the time, they're wrong. My mother kept all the babies well and wouldn't let a doctor near them."

"Didn't Gerry talk to you this morning?" I asked.

"Yes, he did," Charlene said. "But I told him homeopathic remedies never hurt anyone, which is more than you can say for drugs those fancy doctors make you use." She huffed and said triumphantly, "See, you tried to get me in trouble, but it didn't work, did it? Now why don't you go straighten up the mess you made in the baby's room."

I was indignant. "What mess?" In the past few days, I'd folded, hung, and tucked away more things than I had in my entire life—mainly, it's true, because I didn't want to give Charlene an excuse to evict me, but I was proud of my new neatness.

"You didn't make your bed," Charlene said. "And it isn't my job to make it for you."

"It doesn't have to be made every day," I argued. "What sense does it make to cover a bed you're just going to uncover a few hours later?"

"That's how life is. Everything gets done over and over," Charlene said. "You clean a floor even though it's just going to get dirty again, and you feed a baby when it's just going to get hungry again."

Her argument surprised me because it was better than any Jen or Mother had ever made for the neatness habit. "Okay," I agreed, "I'll flip the covers back."

"Do it right. There's no sense if you don't do it right."

Now she was getting bossy, and I wasn't going to let her get away with it. I didn't move. Idly, I started talking, "Is Ina from the agency, Charlene?"

"No."

"Well, how do you know her?"

The question set off sparks. "You're at it again," she said. "You're always after me. I never did anything to you. Why are you always after me?"

Her eyes narrowed in on me in a scary way, like a cat getting ready to pounce. I thought I'd better scuttle out of her way. If Meredith was sick, Gerry would get her to a doctor when he got home. "I guess I'll go over to my friend's house," I said.

"You'd better make your bed first," Charlene commanded. "And get me a diaper from Baby's closet while you're up there." She seemed to think she had control of me now.

"How about a please?" I said with a smile.

She stared at me silently. The stare made me shiver. To keep from annoying her more, I made my bed, brought her the diaper she wanted and took off for Willie's. I wanted to ask him what he thought I should do about Charlene.

Nobody answered the door at the Roses' house. I knocked and rang the bell, but nobody answered.

As I walked home, I tried to decide whether to lay low or keep after Charlene so that she'd act strange enough for Gerry to notice when he got home, which should be soon. Water was running in the bathroom and nobody was around downstairs. The water kept running and running. Was Charlene taking a bath? I got scared for Merry and ran up to find out where she was. The bathroom door was open and Merry was lying naked on the rug next to the tub. Charlene was leaning over the tub adjusting the water.

"Hey," I blurted out. "We have a special sponge mat for the baby so you can bathe her in the kitchen sink."

Merry was waving her hands in the air fretfully and kicking her legs. She still didn't look right to me.

"She's going swimming," Charlene said. "Close the door."

"Swimming? How can she swim? She's a baby."

"That's right. Don't you know that infants are natural swimmers?"

"Not by themselves." Meredith could drown!

"Not by themselves, no," Charlene agreed reasonably. "I'm getting in with her. Close the door now. I'm getting undressed."

"But she might have a fever."

"This'll cool her down. Look, I know what I'm doing even if you don't believe it. You remind me of that woman my stepdaddy married. She didn't think I knew about babies, either. But I *know*."

I blinked. She'd told me something important, but I wasn't sure what. She knew she'd told me something, too, because suddenly she jumped up and pushed me out of the room. Then she locked the door.

The nursery was right across the hall. I sat there on my bed where I could hear if Merry cried. I'd break down the bathroom door if I had to. Why didn't Gerry hurry up and get home? I heard Merry chortle. Good. At least, she was alive. When I'm nervous I eat. But I didn't dare leave to scavenge the kitchen. Instead, I began chewing my fingernails the way Jen does when she's nervous.

Finally, Charlene brought Merry out of the bathroom wrapped in a towel. "She'll sleep now, and tomorrow she'll be fine," Charlene said.

She dressed Merry in a nightshirt and tucked

a blanket around her. The big blue eyes did look brighter, and her soft cheek was cool when I touched it.

"See?" Charlene said to me.

I nodded.

"Good-night and sleep tight, my baby girl," Charlene cooed at Merry.

I stood by the crib after Charlene left, watching Merry fall asleep. Her eyes closed. I tucked my finger into her hand and she gripped it hard. A mushy swelling filled my chest. I loved that little doll-sized bundle so much. But how was I going to protect her?

Through the window above the crib, I saw Charlene walking up the hill. She looked like any ordinary young woman in her jeans with her big drawstring purse slung over her shoulder and her blond hair tied in a tail down her back. "My baby girl," she'd called Meredith. Baby, my baby, and pet names, but did she ever use Meredith's real name? Not that I could remember. Somehow I had to convince my parents that Charlene wasn't ordinary. I had to do it, and soon, because Merry *wasn't* safe with that sneaky woman.

"Case, Jen!" Gerry was shouting.

I went to the top of the stairs to shush him so that he wouldn't wake Meredith. "Jen's not home yet," I said.

"Then you get to hear the good news first." He was beaming.

"You won the sweepstakes?"

"Something like that. I just got a phone call. They want to syndicate one of my comic strips."

"Fantastic. The one about Meredith?"

"No, no. I tossed that stuff out. This was one on suburban living."

I went downstairs to give him a big kiss.

"This is my lucky year," he said. "First my daughter's born, and now a syndicated strip. That means regular money coming in, and who knows, maybe someday even a book."

"You mean your *third* daughter is born," I corrected him. "You already had two."

"Right, you and Jen, a terrific pair of kids." He pinched my cheek gently. "We're going to eat out tonight. I'll call and tell your mother to meet us at a restaurant. When's Jen due home?"

"I don't know." I felt a little odd. Could I love Merry so much and still be jealous of her because she's Gerry's real daughter, not just a stepchild like me? Charlene had loved her stepfather, too. I wondered how she had really felt about her younger brothers or sisters. Her family sounded pretty mixed-up. Maybe she had a reason to be strange. But even if I should be feeling sorry for her, I didn't trust her to take care of my sister.

A few minutes later Jen dragged in and went straight to her bedroom. I was poking through my pitiful collection of clothes looking for something dressy to wear for Gerry's celebration, but I couldn't find anything. Well, a party girl I'm not. I dipped into Jen's room to ask her to lend me something and to talk to her about Charlene. Jen looked awful.

"What's the matter with you?"

"He's going steady with Chrissie. He told me in study hall today. He says I'm too straight for him, too good. What he means is, I'm boring. I told you I was, Case."

"But you aren't. You're a beautiful person. Just because *he* doesn't appreciate you doesn't mean anything. What's so great about Charlie, anyway? You go find a guy who's crazy about you. That'll show him."

I waited for her to tell me I didn't understand, but instead she put her arm around me and said huskily, "Thanks, Case."

It wasn't a good time to bring up Charlene. Jen was in no mood to listen.

She gave me a scoop-neck sweater to wear for the celebration dinner. Gerry whistled when he saw me in it, which made me feel embarrassed and good at the same time.

"It looks better on you than on me," Jen said. "Keep it. You can wear it to the seventh-grade party with the purple heart earrings I gave you for your birthday." The sweater had tiny pink and purple flowers around the neck.

"Oh, Jen. Thank you, thank you, thank you," I said. "You're the best sister. Isn't she, Mother?"

Mother nodded. She even threw in a sort of compliment. What she said was, "You're looking more like thirteen than twelve every day, Case."

"Is that good?" I asked.

"It has to be an improvement," she said. "Twelve's been the worst."

"That's what you said about eleven."

Everybody laughed. Meredith went to dinner with us in her bouncer, but all she did was sleep through the occasion.

"That swim must have really knocked her out," I said.

"Swim?" Mother asked.

We had dessert while I detailed Charlene's baby-rearing methods, including swimming sessions, and that doctors didn't know anything, only Ina did.

Mother looked concerned. "Didn't you talk to her, Gerry?"

"Sure I did. She believes in homeopathic medicine. But she swore she wouldn't give Meredith anything unless she checked it out with us first. And she swore she'd never drive anywhere without strapping Merry in the infant car seat."

"Okay, but I think I'd better have a talk with her, too, and make sure that she understands she has to follow our directions. Her beliefs are her own business, but how she treats Meredith is ours."

Mother must have been thinking about it because on the way home she asked, "Did Charlene ever bring those references we asked her for, Gerry?"

"Sure. She showed me a couple of letters, one from a woman she baby-sat for, and a typed one from a store where she worked. I would've kept them to show you, but she said she needed them back."

"What for?"

"She didn't say. What's the difference?" Gerry said. "Listen, her methods may be a little unorthodox, but she's turned Meredith into a living doll, hasn't she?"

"Umm," Mother said. "I suppose the agency investigated her background. But if her ideas are so bizarre—"

"Look, I'll just tell her we want the baby bathed in the sink on the sponge pad, and that she should call our doctor pronto at the first sign of anything wrong. That's all."

He's too easygoing, I thought, and urged, "You talk to her, Mother, please. Just keep asking her questions." Charlene would have a hard time staying cool if Mother grilled her. If only they could have seen Charlene's face this afternoon after I annoyed her— just that look would have convinced them not to leave Merry in her hands.

Grams called from Cincinnati that night, and I was the one who picked up the phone. "Where were you?" she demanded. "I've been calling and calling." Like Willie, Grams doesn't believe in hellos and goodbyes.

"We were eating dinner out. Gerry sold a comic strip, and it's going to be in papers all over the country."

"Is that so? I hope they'll pay him."

"Sure, they will. He's going to make a fortune. How are you, Grams?"

"There's nothing wrong with me. I don't hear the baby screaming."

"She doesn't anymore. Merry's turned into a

sweetie pie. We got a sitter who tamed her."

"A sitter?"

I explained about Charlene, emphasizing her good points.

"Young and pretty?" Grams asked.

"Well, young and nice looking," I said. Pretty was probably stretching it.

"I don't trust her, from the sound of it," Grams said.

I grinned. Without one clue from me, Grams was already suspicious.

"And you say this sitter keeps the baby quiet? I bet she uses paregoric. Whiskey on a rag, paregoric, coke syrup—those old-fashioned home remedies work on colicky babies, but how safe they are's another thing, especially the paregoric."

"Maybe you should come for a visit," I suggested.

"I'm planning to come and see my newest grand-daughter on my vacation in August."

"August! Merry will be sitting up by then."

"Well, I'm too old to put up with babies much younger." Grams worked as a companion to elderly people. Right now she was with an old man who'd had a stroke and couldn't talk. I bet he itched to tell Grams off. She's bossy.

"Put your mother on, Case."

"Bye, Grams. See you in August," I said.

She must have given Mother an earful because I heard Mother screeching, "We're not giving the baby paregoric." Grams is the only one who can make my mother screech.

102

I still felt bad about not being able to baby-sit with Jason on Saturday, but I wasn't angry at Mother about it anymore. I hoped she'd start quizzing Charlene soon so that I wouldn't have to keep worrying and watching. In fact, I wondered if I ought to keep my appointment with Willie for our after-school dance lesson tomorrow. Unless I could talk him into coming to our house . . . . After all, the baby wasn't screaming anymore.

·NINE·

Willie insisted he had to have privacy for his dance lesson. That meant we went to his house after school Wednesday, which was fine with me because I didn't have to worry about keeping an eye on Charlene for a while. Mother and Gerry had decided he should spend the afternoon at home to see for himself how Charlene was and how she handled Meredith.

While Willie rolled up the area rug in his family room, I gave him a pep talk. "Dancing's natural," I said. "It's just moving to music, basically, which anybody with two good legs and ears can do."

Willie nodded. He got the tape going, but when he got his feet going, too, he looked just like a frozen scarecrow. "Relax," I told him. He didn't. I forgot about steps and tried to make him kind of lean around and bend and shake to the sounds. "Go limp, Willie, go limp," I begged. "Let your body feel the vibrations."

Willie tried. No question, he tried. He flopped around; he sagged like a plastic bag, and if you can imagine a stiff, saggy plastic bag, that was Willie. Somehow his body was tuned wrong.

104

"Look," I told him finally, "when we get to the party, if you don't feel like dancing, we won't, okay?"

"After all the work you put in to teaching me? I'll dance, Case," good old Willie promised me earnestly. "Don't worry. I won't chicken out on you."

My hero! What could I say? I only hoped the gym would be dark Friday night and the floor too crowded for anybody to get a full view of him.

The week of the seventh-grade party was going peacefully. I was being extra careful in school to keep my mouth shut and my feet on the floor around Mrs. Thompson. Mother hadn't mentioned reform school camp again, and though she'd sounded pained telling Gerry about the bleached spot on the nursery rug, she'd let me off on that one, too. In fact, her quiet suffering made me feel more guilty than if she'd yelled at me.

So little happened during Gerry's afternoon with Charlene that he reported she seemed pretty normal to him. Meredith was thriving. She hadn't gotten sick after all and was doing more babbling and squealing than yelling. I thought it was possible, just barely possible, that Charlene wasn't as weird as I'd thought, and I told myself that if she was just *different*, I, of all people, shouldn't criticize her for it. Certainly, she had improved our family life. Gerry went around with a permanent grin and came home early because his work was going so well.

Mother had told him to remind Charlene about the dinner preparation, which was supposed to be part of her job. Awhile before she was due to leave on Wednesday, Gerry offered to watch the baby if Charlene would start dinner for us. She didn't look as if she liked the idea, but she went into the kitchen, with me along to help her find things. That part had been Gerry's suggestion, too.

"You never ate the cauliflower soup I made you," Charlene said to me.

It was still in the refrigerator, getting moldy. Gerry had thought he'd spice it up somehow, but he hadn't gotten around to it.

"Uh . . . I guess it was a little too rich for us," I offered as a polite excuse. I was being very polite and careful around Charlene.

"Wasting food is sinful," she told me.

Charlene took to cooking the way Willie did to dancing. Dinner that night was undercooked rice with canned tuna fish and overcooked broccoli. Even Gerry and I, who'll eat most anything, balked. Luckily, we found a pizza in the freezer.

The next afternoon Gerry suggested Charlene try chicken. "Just bake it plain and maybe make a salad with it," he said. She gave him the narrowed-in glare she usually directed at me. I noticed he flinched.

"I don't think she likes cooking," he whispered to me. Then he carried Merry off to the backyard to try out the basket swing he'd already hung on a tree branch for her, even though she wasn't sitting up by herself yet.

It may have been my fault the chicken was overcooked. Charlene put it in the oven and left. When Gerry asked me how long it had been cooking,

I didn't know, because I'd been giving Willie his last dance lesson before the party. Gerry set the burned pan to soak, and we all sat down to eat as soon as Mother got home.

"So cooking's not her thing," Gerry said while he and I were trying to chew our wooden chicken. Jen had given up. Mother was dousing hers in soy sauce. "But otherwise she's a gem."

Mother nodded. She must have been really hungry that night because she was the only one who finished her chicken.

Merry cooed and chuckled to herself on the blanket that Gerry'd put near us on the kitchen floor. It was funny to watch the blanket go as Merry performed like an energetic inchworm on her back. When she rolled off, Gerry picked her up and held her while he ate. The love he radiated looking down at her was awesome. Well, Meredith was *his* baby, more his than I had ever been or could be. I couldn't blame him for loving her best, but I didn't have to like it.

Friday was so full of sunshine, even the leaves glittered. Andrea came to school hyped about the party and got me going so that I spent the whole social studies period deciding whether to polish my fingernails or not. Andrea's mother was doing hers after school.

In math Andrea dropped a note on my desk that said, "Wear panty hose." Can you imagine? "No way," I wrote back. "It's either ski socks or barefoot." On the way home, I decided barefoot wouldn't be bad, or I could wear my white canvas sandals from last year. Except they were grungy. I planned to wash them and wear them wet if they didn't dry by evening.

That was my last thought about the party because when I walked into the house, there on the floor was Meredith doing her rolling act right toward the open door to the basement. I scooped her up just in time. She was so startled, she began to yell, which brought Charlene charging up the basement stairs.

"What are you doing to the baby?"

"Keeping her from killing herself," I said. "You left the door to the basement open."

"I did not." She slitted her eyes at me, and her mouth went thin. Then she grabbed Meredith as if *I* might be out to harm her.

Annoyed by her turning the tables like that, I insisted, "The door was open, Charlene. You forgot to close it."

She ignored me and kicked the door shut. "There, baby, there, there, love," she comforted Meredith. Cooing, she nestled Meredith under her chin and turned her back on me.

"It's just lucky I got home in time," I said, determined to get Charlene to admit she'd made a mistake.

Meredith's cries were trailing off. "You're still trying to get me in trouble with your parents, aren't you?" Charlene said over her shoulder.

"Well," I said, "she *is* my sister. I don't want anything to happen to her."

"Oh, I bet!" Charlene's eyes scorched me. "I just bet. You'd be glad to have your stepfather to yourself again, wouldn't you?"

"Hey," I said, "speak for yourself, lady."

Lightning flashed in her eyes. "I loved my baby girl. I wasn't jealous of her," she said.

Her baby girl? A sister, I supposed she meant. I shut up. Charlene hadn't admitted anything and she'd made me feel squirmy.

In a singsong voice, Charlene told Meredith, "Up we go now, and we'll swim in the tub because that's what my baby doll likes." With one foot on the stair, she looked at me. "I never told on you about the stain," she said. "But *you* told on me. Well, I hope you're satisfied."

I stood there bewildered, watching her climb up. She'd sounded just like a kid. And even though I knew I'd done the right thing, I was feeling guilty, as if I shouldn't have reported her odd ways to the parents. But that was crazy. I *had* done the right thing.

Downstairs the dryer thumped hollowly in a slow rhythm. I shuddered. When my parents were around, Charlene acted normal. *Acted* was the key word, I suspected. The only one she could be herself with was me because I was just a kid and had no power. I wondered if I could somehow get her agitated long enough for the parents to see her as I saw her.

I didn't polish my nails. I didn't look for panty hose. I just sat in the nursery, listening for any unusual noises from the bathroom, until I heard Gerry come in. Then I rushed downstairs.

"She left the basement door open, and Meredith almost rolled down the stairs," I blurted out. "She won't admit she did it, though."

Gerry put down the plastic bags of groceries he was carrying. "What?"

I started from the beginning and explained in more detail.

"It was accidental, Case. Probably Charlene was as scared of what almost happened as you were." Calmly, he began unloading salad and peaches into the refrigerator.

"But she won't admit she did it."

"Maybe she can't admit it was her fault, even to herself. She's crazy about Meredith."

"She's crazy, all right," I muttered.

"I'm leaving," Charlene said from the kitchen doorway. "The baby's asleep in her crib. She won't be any trouble to you. I take *good* care of her." The way she said it made me think she'd overheard us.

"Of course you do," Gerry reassured her. "You're doing a great job with Meredith."

Charlene accepted the praise with a nod and gave me a smug look. I couldn't believe how good she was at twisting things to her favor.

The phone rang after Charlene left. Andrea wanted to know if her mother should pick up Willie and me. "So the four of us can go in together."

"Okay," I agreed without much enthusiasm. I was still in a turmoil about Charlene.

"What's the matter with you?" Andrea asked.

"I'm tired. I think I'll take a nap instead of polishing my nails."

110

"That's okay," Andrea said. "Your nails are too short, anyway."

Even my friends had to be critical!

Besides wearing the purple heart earrings and the scoop-neck cotton knit sweater, I got Jen to make up my eyes and I used lip gloss that evening. Jen said I looked pretty. Well, of course she'd say that, but, anyway, I looked pretty old in the mirror, almost old enough to be dating. Jen's feet are smaller than mine, but Mother wears my size. She was having a dinner meeting and wasn't home yet. In her closet, I found a pair of dressy sandals with a heel I could manage so long as Willie didn't want to dance much. And if I broke my leg on my first date, well, *that* would make it memorable.

"Gerry," I yelled down to the living room, "can I borrow Mother's shoes for the party?"

"Shhh." He came to the foot of the stairs and put his finger to his lips. "You'll wake up the baby."

"Well, can I?"

"I guess. Sure, go ahead. I'll take the blame if she objects."

He eyed me appreciatively when I got downstairs. "Who gave you permission to grow up so fast?" he asked, and then he said sort of wistfully, "You look a lot like your mother when I first met her."

"Is that good?"

"I thought it was."

Andrea's mother honked for me. Gerry kissed me good-bye with tears in his eyes, which had to mean that he still loved me a little, which made me go off happier than even his compliment had made me.

Andrea and Mason were in the backseat of the car, holding hands. I got in beside her mother in the front, thinking that was pretty bold of Andrea with her mother right there, thinking, also, that Andrea and I are not at all alike. She'd probably be really disappointed in Willie and me as a couple. He never holds my hand, and I only hold his boa constrictor or his guinea pig.

I barely recognized Willie when he got to the car. He was wearing a white shirt and tie like a junior executive, and he looked thin. Either he'd grown in the past four hours, or he had on pants that really fit him.

"You look nice, Willie," I told him.

He grunted and hesitated over whether to get in the front or the back. Andrea scooched closer to Mason. Willie opened the back door and sat next to her. Would you believe it, I felt rejected? I had to tell myself not to be stupid. That's what comes of premature dating.

The seventh-grade party committee had hired a disc jockey who was supposed to put us in a dancing mood and handle the lights and the tape deck. He had the lights and music going in the gym, but he wasn't talking, not a word that would get the kids hanging around the edges of the floor onto it. Maybe he was in a mood of his own; or else he had laryngitis. We four drifted toward the cookies and punch, which were on a paper-covered table, monitored by a pair of ladies from the PTA. We sampled a cookie each, but nobody was very hungry.

"Let's see what games they have in the hall," I suggested as Andrea stared longingly at the empty dance floor.

"Good idea," Willie agreed.

He and I started for the hall with Andrea and Mason tailing us.

Willie won at darts. He wanted to keep playing, but we pried him loose from the prizes, which were jelly beans. Don't ask me why jelly beans. We played a couple of games of Ping-Pong. Then Andrea wanted to play Bingo, but Willie and Mason didn't. So they played Foozball and I stayed with Andrea to play Bingo, which was nice of me because I think it's boring.

We'd used up half the party time and hadn't danced yet. "Somebody *must* be on the dance floor by now," Andrea said.

Willie stiffened in preparation. He was so dignified in his suit that even with Mother's heels on, I didn't feel taller than him, although I was. He and I stalled by eating some more cookies while we watched Andrea and Mason take to the dance floor. Little clumps of dancers were scattered out there now, spread too thin to hide in, but Andrea and Mason didn't need to hide. They looked good.

"Okay, let's go," Willie said.

"We don't have to, Willie."

"Nobody dies from dancing." He took my hand. His felt icy, but he walked me on to the floor, my brave Willie.

Oh, boy! I'd thought he was pretty bad, but I

didn't realize he was a one-man spectacle. Half the dancers turned to watch us. Willie was doing calisthenics, not in time to the music, either. He bent at the knee and jerked up. He flapped his arms. He tilted. And all with his feet clamped in one place on the floor. Somebody snickered. I started talking loud and fast to keep Willie from noticing that he was being noticed.

"Nice party," I said. "I feel older, don't you, Willie? You look older. I like you dressed up. Did you get the shirt just for the party?"

"I'm dancing my best," he said grimly.

"You're doing fine."

"Then why're people laughing at me?"

"They aren't laughing at you."

"They are, too."

"Want to stop?"

"Not in the middle. We gotta wait till the music stops."

"Willie, you're a terrific kid."

"Not a good dancer, though."

"Well, your style's original."

He sighed with relief when he finally allowed himself to walk us off the floor.

"Where'd you learn to dance like that, Willie?" a grinning boy with buckteeth asked him.

"From years of dance class," my Willie snapped back.

We marched out to the hall. "Do you feel like doing more games?" I asked him.

"No." He shook his head. "You can. I'm going to the parking lot to wait until it's time to go home."

"I'll go with you."

It was a warm night. We sat on the planter near the side door. "I'm never going to another dance as long as I live," he said.

"I'm sorry, Willie."

"It's not your fault. It's just I can't dance."

"Maybe if you had a better teacher."

"No," he said.

"We could go back and play darts."

"I'm fine here. You go play. I don't want to ruin your party, Case."

"Oh, who cares about the party? I'd rather be with you," I said.

Willie's eyes widened as if I'd said something amazing. "Really?" he asked, and before I could answer, he leaned over and kissed me right on the lips.

"Willie!" Now I was the one to be amazed.

"What? Did I do something wrong?"

I thought about it. "No. That's okay." I thought some more and almost told him he was better at kissing than dancing, but I didn't want to trigger a repeat performance. My lips were still tingling. Besides, I hadn't expected to be kissed, not for years, and then not by Willie. I hoped it hadn't ruined our friendship.

"It's a nice night," I said. "Do you know any star constellations?"

He taught me how to find Draco, the dragon, that night. It kind of winds between the Big and Little Dippers.

Andrea's mother picked us up on time, and when Andrea asked where we'd disappeared to, I said casually, "We were out in the parking lot, necking." Her mother whipped around and stared at me, but Andrea looked impressed, and Willie grinned with satisfaction.

Meredith was crying, and Mother was trying to get her back to sleep when I went up to bed. "I wish Charlene stayed nights, too," Mother said.

Late as it was, I didn't want to start arguing with her about Charlene. I was getting good at keeping my mouth shut.

Yawning, Mother asked, "How was your party, Case?"

"Nice."

"Oh, I'm so glad." She sounded sincere.

"You go to bed," I said. "I'll get Meredith to sleep." I did, too, and I didn't let myself think about Charlene. I had the whole weekend to do that. Meanwhile, I could relax and recall my first date and how well it had turned out, after all.

·TEN·

My invitations to Tippy's party were heart shaped, naturally. Jen ran them off on her computer, and Willie helped me cut them out. Andrea's job was to hand them out Monday morning and warn everybody in our class not to tell Mrs. Thompson about the party. We picked Andrea to do the inviting because she was still passing as a regular kid, even though she'd been hanging out with Willie and me.

"Kids might not come if they know the party's my idea," I confessed to her.

She grinned at me as if that was no news to her. I was thrilled. I mean, she knew I was an oddball and didn't care. That means she's really a friend, which makes two for me. I'm practically popular!

The party was supposed to be a surprise to Tippy, too, but somebody must have slipped and told her. She sat down next to me in language arts, and leaning close, as if she were helping me with my work, she whispered, "Case, I think it's super of you to want to give me a party, but I can't let you get in more trouble with Mrs. Thompson on my account."

"Don't worry," I said. "We're having it after school, not during, and outside on the patio. It's legal."

"Is it?" She thought about it and then said reluctantly, "Well, all right. I'll take a chance and come."

"Take a chance?" I'd thought I was the only risk taker. "You mean, *you* could get in trouble?"

"Sure. Mrs. Thompson has to do my final evaluation—like giving me a report card? But if the party's a surprise, if I didn't know about it—" Her big blue eyes were checking to make sure I understood. "I don't think she could blame me."

"No problem. You don't know about it, and I'll tell Willie and Andrea. They're my committee."

She gave me a mischievous smile and winked and moved to someone who really did need help with the worksheet.

Meredith was on a blanket on the grass, with Charlene beside her in a lawn chair, when I got home from school. Charlene was sewing something as I came across the yard, but she stuffed it in a plastic bag, so that her hands were empty when I got close.

"Hi-ya, Merry mite." I scooped up my little sister and smooched her on the neck. She giggled, and I told her what a cutie pie she was. "What are you making, Charlene?"

"Nothing."

I saw a scrap of flowered baby flannel on the grass and wondered if she was pregnant and didn't want

118

us to know. Unless she was making something for Meredith. But then, why hide it?

"Would you bring me a warm, damp washcloth, please? Baby's dirty," Charlene said.

I didn't know whether she was trying to get rid of me, or just got a charge out of sending me on errands, but it was no big deal either way; so I went. I detoured past the refrigerator, ate a blueberry yogurt, then dutifully dampened Meredith's washcloth and took it back outside.

Merry was looking cross-eyed at a blade of grass stuck in her fist. I made googly eyes at her, and she stuck her tongue out at me.

"You mutt," I teased her. "Show some respect for your big sister."

"*Your* big sister went to her room. She says she doesn't feel well," Charlene said. "I wanted to make her some chamomile tea, but she said it wouldn't help. I don't see how she knows that without trying it."

"Jen likes to be left alone when she doesn't feel well," I said. "She's probably got cramps from her period or something."

"She should have told me. I can fix that, too," Charlene said.

"From that green plastic kit? You carry it with you?"

"It's got homeopathic remedies, nothing artificial, just nature's own remedies that people have used for generations."

I nodded. I wanted to ask her how come, if they worked, doctors didn't prescribe them, but I was afraid of irritating her. Instead, I said, "I guess I'll go see if Jen wants anything."

Her bedroom door was shut. "You need some aspirin?" I called to her.

"No, thanks."

I opened the door and peeked inside. Jen was coiled up in bed like a new garden hose. "Are you head sick or stomach sick?" I asked her.

"Heartsick."

"Can I come in?"

"Okay," she said in a sad little voice.

"You got kicked off a computer for losing a disc?" I asked to get a rise out of her. She shook her head. "You failed a math test?" Another shake. "Charlie still?"

"I saw him at his locker, kissing Chrissie. Everybody was looking at them, and they didn't care."

"So what? You're finished with him, anyway."

"He's finished with me, you mean," Jen said. I realized her eyes were on his picture. She had it in a plastic, stand-up frame on her night table.

I picked up the photo. "What a cocky-looking guy. Makes me want to punch him out," I said.

Jen smiled, as I'd hoped she would, and took the frame away from me. "I quiver every time I see him, Case. I can't help it. The only time I'm not thinking about him is computer club."

"Then what you should do," I advised, "is tear up his picture and go to work on a computer program so awesome it'll make you rich and famous. So then he'll read about you in the papers and wish he'd hung on to you so you could buy him a fancy sports car and send him to orthodontia school."

Jen laughed, then said, "But, Case, you can't believe how hard it is to stop being crazy about someone." She pulled the picture out of the frame and sniffled over it for a while.

I offered, "Did I tell you what Willie did to me at the seventh-grade party?"

"What?" She didn't sound interested.

"He got me alone in the parking lot and embraced me passionately."

"What?" This "what" sounded startled. Now I had her attention.

"My first kiss, Jen! And I'm only twelve years old. Right on the lips, too." I tapped the very spot.

She chuckled. It was the sound of success, since I was trying to cheer her up. "Really?" she said. "Did you like it?"

"Well . . ." I considered. "It wasn't bad. Sort of tingly, but I'm in no rush to go for seconds. Do you think I'm abnormal?"

Jen chuckled again. "You're fine."

"It's great having a big sister I can talk to," I said. Then she let me kiss her, which doesn't happen often, and by the time I left her, she was tearing up Charlie's picture.

I was feeling good, really good, until I got downstairs and saw Gerry aiming his camera at Meredith in the backyard.

"Want me to get her to laugh for you?" I asked him.

121

"Would you, honey? My great-aunt down in Florida wants pictures of Meredith. I guess she doesn't believe I really have a kid."

"What aunt down in Florida? Did you ever send her pictures of Jen and me?"

"She never asked for any." He was embarrassed. "She's just an old lady, Case. I do my duty by her on her birthday once a year. She's not a big item in my life."

But she wanted a picture of his daughter, his real daughter, not his stepchild. *Twang* went the jealousy chord.

"Hey," Gerry said. "What's with the long face? You know how special you are to me, don't you?"

"Uh-huh," I agreed, and walked away, forgetting I'd promised to make Merry smile. I didn't want to listen to nice things he didn't mean. I thought about Jen's having to accept that Charlie wouldn't be her one and only. Now it was my turn. I had to swallow that I wasn't the big deal in Gerry's life anymore. Jen was right about how hard it was.

Andrea wasn't in school Tuesday. I panicked. Wednesday was party day, and Andrea had all the money we'd collected for soda and chips. Her mother, the only nonworking mom we had, was supposed to be delivering the heavy stuff to school at three o'clock. I was going to bake brownies, and Willie was baking oatmeal cookies, but without the soda, all we'd have was water, and without Andrea, the party might flop.

I raised my hand to ask Mrs. Thompson's permission to make a phone call in the office.

"Whom do you need to call, Case?"

I could have lied and said, my mother, but I didn't. I said, "I have to ask Andrea something important."

"It can certainly wait until after school," Mrs. Thompson said frostily.

Willie made the call for me during science. Mr. Sobel didn't even ask him why he wanted to leave the room. Mr. Sobel's a nice teacher.

"It's okay," Willie told me when he got back. "She's sick, but her mother's buying the party stuff and says Andrea'll be well enough to come tomorrow."

"Whew! That's a relief."

"It's supposed to rain tomorrow," Willie said.

"It can't. It won't, Willie."

"I listened to the weather radio this morning. Ninety percent chance of rain."

"Umbrellas?" I suggested feebly.

He just looked at me.

"We'll think of something," I said. "We've been planning this party for so long. We can't give it up now."

"I could easily," he said.

"Getting in trouble worries you, huh?"

"If I was really worried about getting in trouble, I'd never've picked you for a friend," he said, and got to work on his lab notebook.

The house was so full of silence it made me nervous when I got home that afternoon. I tiptoed around calling, "Charlene?" No Charlene. No Merry. No one. I told myself Charlene had just taken Merry for a walk or something, but I finished off a carton of ice cream *and* my math homework, and they still weren't home. It got to be half past four. Charlene never worked past five. Finally, I couldn't stand it anymore, and I called Gerry. He took his calls at the dress shop.

"What do you mean, they're not home? Where are they?"

"That's what I don't know," I said.

"Didn't Charlene leave you a note?"

"No."

"That's odd. Unless she had to rush Meredith to the hospital—an accident or maybe the baby took sick."

He sounded so scared that I had to take a turn being reasonable. "Then she would've called you, or Mother, right? Besides, Charlene doesn't believe in doctors; so she probably doesn't trust hospitals, either."

"Who knows?" Gerry said. "She's got some funny ideas." I was glad he'd noticed. He told me he'd be right home.

He was, too, like in seven minutes flat. "Not yet?" he asked, looking like a wild man with the wisps of hair around his bald dome sticking out and his eyes round with worry. "Come on, get in the car."

"Where are we going?" I asked.

"I don't know. We'll cruise around looking and then go to the police."

"If she came in her friend's truck this morning, maybe we should check the park," I said. It was another warm, breezy afternoon.

"Good idea."

Gerry babbled, as he drove, about how he wished Charlene had a phone. "I asked for her phone number," he said, "and she said she didn't have one. All I have is an address. I don't even know where the street is. What I need is a local map. We'll go to the park, then the police."

He wasn't thinking very clearly, I realized. What he should have done was leave me home in case Charlene returned and also to alert Jen and Mother to what was going on, but I didn't say anything because we were more than halfway to the park.

Lots of little kids were in the Tiny Tot Playground, which featured horse swings and elephant and chicken slides and miniature merry-go-rounds and a sandbox. Merry was too young even for a basket swing, but there she was with Charlene on a bench full of waiting mothers chatting to each other.

"Thank God!" Gerry said when I pointed them out. He stopped the car and just stared. Then he said, "We'd better turn around and go home now. I don't want Charlene thinking I don't trust her. I'll talk to her later about going off without letting us know where."

"I bet she doesn't realize how late it is," I said.

"Right. I don't think she owns a watch. I could give her an old one of mine."

"You're going to give Charlene a watch?" I couldn't believe it. "If I'd gone off with the baby without leaving a note, you'd have killed me."

Gerry took a deep breath. "You're right, but the thing is, Charlene's our salvation. Now that we've got her, we don't want to lose her."

"Gerry," I said in a burst of inspiration. "You know what? *I* could be Merry's baby-sitter this summer when I'm home from school, and then we wouldn't need Charlene. You could even save money. I'll work cheap."

"You're a good kid, and I appreciate the offer, but twelve's kind of young for a full-time job. Besides, what would we do in the fall when you go back to school?"

"Look for a regular, ordinary-type baby-sitter."

"From what my friendly dress shop landlady tells me, it's tough to find a good one. We've been lucky."

"But she doesn't like me, Gerry."

"She doesn't like any of us except Meredith."

"But I'm around her the most."

"And this summer. . . . Yeah, you'll be home all day." He raised his eyebrows and pushed out his lips, thinking. "Well, you can spend most of your time at that pool we're joining."

Charlene stood up with the baby in her arms, apparently saying good-bye to her companions.

"We better get out of here before she sees us," Gerry said, and took off for home.

It looked like this was going to be my summer for swim practice, or else for tending to little animals at Willie's house, unless I could talk Andrea into exploring Livingston by bike with me. One thing I sure wasn't going to want to do was hang around home with Charlene there.

·ELEVEN·

It didn't just rain Wednesday; it gushed water. At every lightning flash and thunder roar Willie shot me a reproachful glance, as if the weather were my fault. Well, he *had* warned me about it. Andrea was too busy blowing her nose and sniffling to care about what was going to happen after school, but the kids who had already paid for their share of Tippy's party kept asking if we were really going to do it. "Sure," I said each time. At noon, Willie and Andrea and I huddled around our sandwiches conferring while the sky cracked open and shook the big glass windows in the cafeteria.

"We can hold it under the overhang between the new wing and the gym," I said.

"That's *in* the school," Willie reminded me.

"In emergencies, you can't stick to the rules, Willie."

"You think the principal will agree? Or Mrs. Thompson?"

"Oh, come on. Now that we've gone this far, let's go for it."

Willie wrinkled his nose unhappily, but he didn't say no.

"It'll be awfully wet," Andrea said. "That roof is open on both sides."

"Let's go check it out now," I said.

We sneaked into the empty gym and peeked out at the concrete breezeway between it and the new wing. Luckily, the rain was coming from behind, leaving a bedroom-size area dry.

"Too small," Willie said.

"But a lot of kids won't come because of the rain," I pointed out. "And actually, a small party's more fun. We can still play games and have the music and talk."

Willie looked doubtful, but Andrea said, "Don't forget the dancing. That's what Mother's bringing the tape deck for."

"You can't feel like dancing with your cold," I said.

"I always feel like dancing," Andrea said, and sniffed hard.

At the end of the last class she was to teach us, Tippy made a tearful good-bye speech. We all cheered, and after the bell rang and we were dismissed, a few kids handed her little gifts and notes. I hadn't finished the pillow I'd started for her, but I figured the party would be my gift. She was on her way to the parking lot when I stopped her to say we were still having it.

"What?"

"The party for you, Tippy. Don't you remember?"

"But, Case, it's pouring."

"Not to worry. Just follow me." She groaned and protested, but Andrea and Willie came by toting the soda and bags of stuff from Andrea's mother's car.

"You got to come, Tippy," Willie said. So she gave in and followed us.

Only about half the class had stayed, which was fine with me, because we could fit under the overhang with enough room to move around a little. Andrea and I got a table from the gym for the refreshments. Everyone fell on the cookies, brownies and soda, gorging cheerfully, while Willie helped me string up my hearts sign with masking tape and Andrea put some music on the tape deck.

The kids who had stayed were either girls who had a crush on Tippy and wanted to grow up to look just like her, or the boys Tippy couldn't control in class. Don't ask me what made *them* stay after they'd given her such a rotten time with spitball wars and desk-banging concerts and wastebaskets that accidentally on purpose got knocked over. Maybe they just liked parties.

"Let's play charades," I suggested. Nobody heard me. I was about to yell above the noise when Andrea blew her nose one last time and began dancing with Mason. A circle formed around them.

Meanwhile, I saw Willie frowning. "Those guys aren't here to dance," he muttered to me.

Our three class hoods were there at the refreshment table, even though they hadn't paid. I considered going over and telling them to pay or go, but I didn't want to give them an excuse to start a riot.

A boy asked Tippy to dance. She shook her head. Her eyes kept going to the hoods, who were guzzling soda straight from the bottles. She looked scared.

"Tippy couldn't handle them in class. What's going to happen now?" Willie said.

"Will you stop it? You're making me nervous," I told him.

The three party crashers suddenly took off into the rain around the corner of the auditorium with extra bottles of soda in their arms.

"Good riddance," I said. We had too many bottles, anyway.

More kids were dancing now, and Tippy finally was persuaded. Somebody opened a bottle of soda that fizzed all over the walkway.

"I'll bring a rag and mop it up tomorrow morning," I told Willie, the worrier, before he could say anything.

Just then we heard the crash: glass breaking, not thunder. Everybody ran out into the rain to see. The hoods were disappearing off school grounds as fast as they could run. They'd left a jagged hole smack through the middle of a big gym window.

Willie groaned on one side of me. Andrea said, "Oh, no!" on the other. A couple of minutes later, we three were the only ones left at the site of the party. Tippy had taken her gifts, said, "Thanks, anyway. I'll never forget you kids," and hurried off into the rain as if she were escaping the scene of a crime.

I pulled down the WE LOVE TIPPY heart sign I'd

worked so hard on, and Andrea and Willie and I cleaned up as best we could. Some soda was left over, but no cookies or brownies. We lugged all the garbage to the dumpster, including the sign, and waited for Gerry to come drive us home.

"She looked sort of sick when she left," Andrea said.

"Well, we cleaned up everything except for the broken window and the spilled soda," I said.

"What makes me mad," Willie grumbled, "is she wasn't worth the trouble we're going to get in for this. She wasn't even a very good teacher."

"Don't worry," I promised. "You and Andrea won't get in trouble. It was my idea. I pushed you into it, and I'll take the blame."

Neither of them objected, which meant I was stuck with my noble offer. No matter. Spreading the blame wouldn't make Thompson and the principal go any easier on me.

"So how did the party go?" Gerry asked when we had all settled in to the car.

"So-so," I said. He didn't yet know we hadn't had permission for this caper. Could I be sent to reform school for giving an illegal party? Reform summer camp, probably. I'd find out after tomorrow morning when they discovered that window.

We got home, and I dripped rain water over the kitchen floor while Gerry stowed the leftover soda in the garage. Charlene was sitting there, ready to leave, with her sewing bag and purse beside her. Merry was asleep on her lap. I dried my hands and face and reached for Merry. Instantly, Charlene put her arm protectively around the baby and said to me, "Look at the mess you made on the floor with your muddy sneakers."

"Okay, okay. I'll wipe it up." I dried the floor with paper towels, dropped them in the garbage, and noticed scraps of pink terry cloth there.

"What are you sewing, Charlene?" I came right out and asked her. "Can I see it?"

"I'm not sewing anything."

I looked at the scraps. Pinked edges don't come by themselves. "Looks like you're making something for a baby," I said. "Is it a surprise for Meredith?"

She didn't answer me. Then she blurted out, "For *my* baby."

"You have one?"

"Yes, I have a baby."

"How come you never mentioned that before?" I asked curiously.

"How come you're so nosy?"

I turned away from her slit-eyed look, feeling bad. Charlene was right to think I was a pest. And Willie was right. I'd been stupid to get in trouble for Tippy just because she was cute and lively and Mrs. Thompson was such a pill. Tippy hadn't been a very good teacher, and she hadn't been my friend.

Feeling low, I went to bed early that night. Meredith was still awake in her crib. Without Charlene there to stop me, I took my baby sister into my bed and cuddled her. Her tiny fingers clutched at my arm, and she gave me a toothless grin. Amazing how that cheered me up. I entertained her with a story about a little mousie in a little housie while she gurgled happily at my nonsense and tried to grab my lips.

It was worse than I'd expected the next morning. Mrs. Thompson didn't let me get to my seat in homeroom before pinning me to the chalkboard.

"Whose idea was that party, Case?" I could tell by the ice in her eyes that she knew it was mine. So I admitted it.

"And who else was involved?" she asked.

"Nobody."

"According to the janitor, some mother brought the soda bottles that smashed the gym windows. Was that your mother?"

"No. I asked a friend of mine for a favor."

"Willie?"

"No. Willie wanted me to forget the party because it was against the rules."

"But you, of course, are above rules."

I couldn't resist saying, "Just dumb ones."

"And do you still think they're so dumb?"

"No," I said reluctantly, "but I didn't throw any soda bottles."

"Maybe not, but you were the instigator."

"I'm sorry things got out of hand. I really am."

"This time, Case, sorry will not do. If I had my way, you'd be suspended from school for the rest of the year. I don't have the authority to do that, but I can banish you from my class and from all year-end activities, like the Field Day tomorrow. I've put up with your miserable behavior long enough."

The principal wasn't too thrilled with me, either. "What am I going to do with you, Case?" His square, plain face studied me sadly.

"Mrs. Thompson's already put me in solitary."

"I know. She wants you out of her room. Well, the only place I can put you is the library. You'd better concentrate on doing your work there. If you try using it as a social center, you'll find yourself spending the summer here in my office with me."

"The broken window really wasn't my fault," I said.

"Yes, well, I've already gotten the names of the culprits, and they'll pay for it."

"*They* didn't get kicked out of class, though," I said bitterly.

"Mrs. Thompson considers you the worst offender because you organized the party," the principal said. "I've got to call your parents in again."

"What?" I squawked. "Kicking me out of class isn't enough?"

"Afraid not." He looked at me solemnly.

"But what'd I do besides make a party for a student teacher? Is that so terrible?"

"You won't abide by the rules of a reasonable institution, namely, this school. That may not be terrible, but it's bad enough."

I argued that the rules weren't reasonable, but he said the evidence was against me. The party *had* gotten out of hand. "And your past record is against you," he added.

He tried getting hold of my parents, but Mother wasn't in her office and Dad's landlady in the dress shop didn't answer. "I'll try again this afternoon," Mr. Hayes said, and shipped me off to my lonely carrel at the back of the library because English came next.

I hadn't gotten any friendly vibes from him at all. He'd probably decided I was just a pain in his neck.

It was the longest, most boring period of the year, sitting there alone in my three-sided cell doing subject-verb agreement exercises. I filled up time decorating the borders of my assignment with hearts— sighing, lonely, wistful hearts holding drooping flowers. I was hoping my hearts would reach Mrs. Thompson's, and she'd let me out of solitary. Instead, I got a note from her at lunch that I should stop messing up the margins of my papers and leave room for her corrections.

On the bus going home, Andrea thanked me for keeping her out of it. Willie asked if I wanted to come over to his house and play a game or pet Zeus or something.

"What I'd better do is go home and get my defense down in writing, in case my parents are too mad to let me speak."

"Good idea," Willie said. "Want me to help?"

"Sure."

Andrea sneezed into her last tissue. "I'd help, too, but you don't need any more of my germs," she said. We didn't argue; she was right.

The house felt empty again. I led Willie straight to the refrigerator, hoping to find something decent

135

in it. Willie's refrigerator was always well-stocked. Ours was only if Gerry had just been food shopping. Treats disappeared first and fast.

"So where's this reformed baby sister of yours?" Willie asked as I mixed raspberry preserves into plain yogurt, which was all I could find.

"I don't know. It's sunny again. Maybe Charlene took Merry to the park or something."

"It's a nice walk to the park," Willie said. "Just over a mile. I clocked it."

"You feel like going there, Willie? We could get a ride back with Charlene. She must have the truck if she went that far with the baby."

"What about your defense?"

"No problem. I'll carry a notepad, and we'll write it in the park."

We had a great discussion as we hiked up the hill and along the shoulder of the main road, past the shopping center where Gerry had his office, past more residential streets and through a shortcut Willie knew. It was about whether punishing people did them any good. Willie didn't believe punishment improved wrongdoers. I said the whole system was wrong.

"All those teachers and principals spend their time thinking up punishments. Why don't they come up with rewards that make being good worthwhile—like skipping your least favorite subject, or getting a candy bar or a tree planted in your honor or even a geranium?"

"Somehow, I can't see Mrs. Thompson giving you a geranium, Case." Willie laughed as if the idea were hilarious. I shoved him with my shoulder and he shoved me back.

Charlene wasn't socializing with the young mothers on the bench this afternoon, and I didn't see her truck in the parking lot. "Too bad. We're going to have to walk home," I said. I wasn't alarmed. Not a bit. Not after the other day when she hadn't been where I expected and I'd dragged Gerry out to search for her and Merry.

"So let's sit somewhere and write up those arguments," Willie said.

"Okay, as soon as I ask them if anyone saw her today."

I approached three women on a bench outside the Tiny Tot Playground. The oldest one had a baby sleeping in a stroller. Next to her was a teenage girl with a baby on her lap. A big woman at the end had long black hair down to her waist and shorts showing off enormous white legs.

"Hi," I greeted them. "Could you tell me if Charlene was here with my baby sister today?"

"*Your* baby sister?" The one with the long black hair sounded surprised. "I didn't know Charlene had an older kid, too."

"Hmm?" I asked.

"We thought from what she said that Baby was her first."

"Her first what?"

"Her first child." The woman with the long black hair set each word down slowly as if I might be retarded. I guess that's how I sounded to her.

"Merry's not Charlene's child," I said. "She's just taking care of her while my parents work."

"No kidding!" the older woman said. She had a deep laugh.

"But Merry's not what Charlene calls her kid. 'Baby' is what she calls her," the girl in the middle argued. "And she looks just like Charlene. We even said how much alike they look. *You* don't look like Baby at all."

"I look like my mother. Merry takes after her father. But listen, was Charlene here or not?"

The older woman shook her head. "Not today."

I swallowed hard. Where was Charlene, and what'd she mean by pretending to be Merry's mother? Unless . . . Charlene had told me the other day that she had a baby of her own. Maybe it *was* her own child she called "Baby" and brought to the park. No. She took care of Meredith during the day. Wherever she left her own baby, it had to be Meredith she brought to the park. I wondered if the woman Charlene called Ina took care of Charlene's baby during the day. But why hadn't Charlene mentioned her baby before? Maybe she'd just invented a baby, her baby, when I asked about what she was sewing. I wouldn't be surprised if she had. She was a sly one, like about that spot on the rug. I was pretty sure she'd been the one who'd knocked the paint jar over by accident. Then she'd blamed it on me so that she wouldn't get in trouble with Mother.

"Thanks," I said over my shoulder to the women, who were talking among themselves about whether

Charlene's "Baby" was her baby or not. Then, grabbing Willie by the arm, I walked him out of the park.

"Something's really wrong," I said once we were out of earshot. "Charlene's been telling people Merry's her baby, and not even using her right name." Charlene never used Meredith's name, I recalled with a shiver.

"Maybe Charlene wants a baby of her own," Willie said.

"She told me she already has one. Do you think that's where she went with Meredith? To wherever her own baby is?"

"Beats me. Want to go back to your house and see if she's back?"

We walked home so fast that we were puffing and sweaty by the time we'd reached my house. I searched it. No Charlene. No baby sister, either. I called Gerry.

"We've been through this once already," he said wearily. "Why do you have to make a drama out of everything, Case? She probably neglected to leave a note again. I'll give her some grief about that. Don't worry."

I had the feeling that he thought I was just trying to get Charlene in trouble. Then I imagined what he'd think after my principal called and told him what a rotten kid I am. "Okay," I said, giving up. "If you're so sure nothing's wrong, okay. I'll just wait here and hope Charlene brings Merry back, or Baby, which is what Charlene calls her to her friends. She claims Merry's her child. Did you know that?"

I was trying to alarm him enough so he'd call the

police, but all he said was, "Sit tight. I'll be home soon."

I hung up, discouraged. "He wasn't even listening to me, Willie."

"Calm down," Willie kept saying to me, "calm down."

"Something's wrong. I know it's wrong." I thought of what Willie had said about Charlene's wanting a baby. Suppose she didn't really have one of her own, but wanted one so bad, so bad that she would pretend ours was hers. Suppose she wanted one of her own so bad that she was willing to *steal* ours. I jumped to my feet. "I'm calling the police myself," I said.

"Wait. Your father'll get here soon. Let him call," Willie urged.

I got another idea. "All right. Then what I'll do is call the agency we got Charlene from. They must know how to reach her, and they'll be closed by the time Gerry gets here. It's quarter of five already." I pulled over the Rolodex to look for the telephone number and dropped it on the floor because my hands were shaking so much. Then I couldn't find the number right away because I didn't know the name of the agency. I had to start at the beginning of the alphabet, hoping the name would have a clue in it, like Child Care or Home Helpers.

At ten minutes to five I found something called Helping Hands. "Got it," I said.

"Let me make the call," Willie said. "I know what to say."

He was clever. "I'm looking for Charlene," he said

when someone answered the phone. "She took care of me while my mother was sick last fall, and I need to ask her something."

He put his hand over the receiver. "What's her last name?"

I bit my lower lip, thinking hard, but I didn't know. "Hold on," I whispered, and dashed to the bulletin board. There it was in Gerry's handwriting, Charlene Bickle, with an address but no phone number.

Willie relayed the name to the woman in the agency. "Nobody?" he said. "But I know Charlene works for your agency. You sent her to us." He shook his head, listened, shook his head some more, thanked the person he was talking to and hung up.

"She says she's the manager and knows everybody who works for her, and doesn't know anyone named Charlene Bickle, not even anyone named Charlene. I don't think she was just putting me off. She sounded sorry about it. Now what?"

I didn't know what. I was dizzy with terror. "Merry!" I wailed. "Where did she take you?"

·TWELVE·

I was so jittery that by the time Gerry got home, after picking Jen up from her four o'clock dentist appointment, I'd finished off three stale doughnuts straight from the freezer and was still hungry. Willie hadn't wanted any frozen doughnuts. Well, he wasn't as nervous as I was.

"So, is everything all right?" Gerry asked hopefully.

"Everything's terrible," I said. "They're not here."

He flinched.

Jen said, "Oh, my God!" and began to chew her fingernails. At least they're not fattening.

"We called the agency to find out how to reach Charlene, and the manager said nobody by that name worked for her," Willie told Gerry.

"That must be a mistake." Gerry took the Rolodex and dialed the same number we'd just tried. Nobody answered.

"They close at five," I told him, "which is why we called."

"I'd better call the police." Gerry sounded scared now.

Willie went home after I promised to call him when we got Meredith back. I leaned on Gerry's shoulder while he spoke to the police. They insisted he make his report in person at the station. "You better go with me, Case," he said after he hung up. "I'll need you."

We hugged each other comfortingly and went, leaving Jen at home in case Charlene came back with Merry, and to wait for Mother.

On the way to the police station, I told Gerry my theory about Charlene wanting a baby of her own, and I said, "Even if she kidnapped Meredith, at least we know she'll take good care of her. Because she really does love babies. All we have to do is find her." I was trying to make him feel better, but he got more and more agitated.

"You told us she was weird, but I didn't want to see it," he said, and then he burst out with, "I can't believe I put my child into the hands of a complete stranger without checking her out. How could I have been so stupidly trusting?"

"Mother didn't check, either," I reminded him. "And she's the practical one." He didn't even notice that I'd insulted him.

"Some parents we are!" he muttered. "So long as Merry wasn't screaming in our ears, we didn't ask. We didn't want to know. Why didn't I—"

"Gerry," I interrupted him, "you have Charlene's address. Did you bring it?"

"Her address? Yes, right. She gave it to me. Where did I put it?"

"On the bulletin board."

He made a screeching turn, raced us back home and left me in the car with the motor running while he dashed into the house. It was after six by the time we finally got to the police station. By then the doughnuts had become bricks in my stomach.

The officer we talked to looked like my school principal, square-faced with wavy gray hair and frown lines. He listened patiently to Gerry, then wanted to know what information we had on Charlene.

"Just her name and address," Gerry admitted.

"Date of birth, phone number, driver's license and social security numbers, references?"

Gerry shook his head and looked embarrassed. "She's been working for us only a couple of weeks. Uh, she gave us some forms that we filled out for the agency, but she took them back. I should have made copies. Won't her address help?" I grabbed his hand and squeezed it because I was afraid he'd cry.

The officer, Sergeant Cullen, studied a map of Essex County. He kept studying it and studying it. Finally he asked, "Sure you've got it spelled right? There's no such street in that town. Unless it's one of these new subdivisions. Hard to keep up-to-date on those. Or she could have given you a phony address, phony name, too, for that matter."

"But the agency sent her," Gerry protested.

"That's something to go on," Sergeant Cullen said.

"Except they say they don't know her," I put in, and told him about the phone call.

144

He looked at me hard. "That your own idea to call the agency?" he asked.

I nodded, and he nodded and took down the name of the manager Willie had spoken to.

Next he wanted a physical description of Charlene and the baby, but he wrote down what we told him so slowly that I had an urge to give his pen a shove. All the while his pen was creeping along the black lines of the form, Charlene was speeding away with my sister. I had to grip the arms of my chair to keep myself from jumping up to chase after her.

Gerry swallowed dryly, and his jaw twitched as his eyes followed the sergeant's pen. The slow motion was getting to him, too.

"Did Charlene have her friend's pickup with her today?" I asked Gerry.

"Pickup?" the sergeant asked alertly. "What year and make?"

"It's an old blue Chevy with dented rear fenders," Gerry said. "I'm not sure what year it is. Can you remember, Case?"

"Me? I'm not good at cars."

Gerry kept apologizing about not knowing the license plate number, but he identified the pickup as a '64 when the sergeant showed him pictures.

What *did* we know, I asked myself. I thought about what the women at the playground had told me. "Charlene tells strangers Meredith's her own child," I mentioned to Sergeant Cullen.

His head snapped up. Suddenly, he looked really concerned. He asked for a picture of Charlene and one of the baby. Gerry had a photo of Merry in his wallet, but we didn't have any of Charlene.

"We'll have the bus and rail stations alerted in case your sitter ditched the truck," the sergeant told us. But he warned, "This is a densely populated area. Easy to fade into the woodwork around here. Or she could have driven to some other state."

"But—then you think my daughter was kidnapped?" Gerry asked.

"It's too soon to conclude that, but it's a possibility. We'll check the hospitals, also." He stood. So we did, too.

"That's it?" Gerry asked anxiously.

"For now. We've got enough to start with. If you discover anything else when you get home, be sure and call." Sergeant Cullen gave Gerry a fatherly pat on the back. "Take it easy. Worrying never pays."

"But you'll get her back?" Gerry begged.

"We'll do our best," the sergeant said. To my amazement, he turned to me then and said, "You'd make a good detective, young lady. You're a sharp one."

"It's Case who smelled a rat," Gerry said. "She tried to tell us Charlene was weird."

"Weird? How?" the sergeant asked me.

"Well, like the way she hated answering questions and got mad at me when I asked her any, and the way she handled the baby, like letting her lie on the floor and swim and—"

"Some of Charlene's methods were unorthodox, but Meredith certainly seemed to react well to them,"

Gerry said defensively.

The sergeant nodded. "Uh-huh. Well, anything else you can think of that might give us a clue, you be sure and call in. Or if you hear from the sitter. If she wants ransom, you'll hear from her. Meanwhile, we'll send out an all-points bulletin on her and the baby." As he spoke he was ushering us toward the door.

We drove home in a dazed silence. I was wishing it was a mistake, and Merry would be there when we got back. Somehow I knew she wouldn't be.

Mother fell into Gerry's arms as he walked in the door. "Why didn't we call the agency when we hired her?" Mother cried. It was her turn for regrets. "Those forms Charlene had us fill out—we should have mailed them in, not just handed them back to her. And her pay—Gerry, I made the checks out to *her*, not to the agency, and it didn't even strike me as odd that we had no contact with them except through Charlene. Those references could so easily have been faked. How could I have been so careless with my own child's well-being?"

She gasped at the news that Charlene had given us a false address.

"I can't believe we didn't even take down her social security number," Gerry said.

"What's the difference? She could have faked it, too," I said to comfort them, but they just moaned in unison.

Jen heated up some canned soup for supper. Mother and Gerry sat down at the kitchen table, still

147

giving themselves a hard time about how irresponsible they'd been until Jen cried, "Please stop yelling at yourselves. *Please.*"

"Let's try and think of things to tell the police," I said. "I remember Charlene's friend's name. It's Ina, and maybe they'd like to know that Charlene shopped at a natural foods store."

"Case, please," Mother said, impatient as ever with my ideas. "That's not what they need to know. The agency—Charlene *must* have had some connection with that agency or how would she get our address?"

Gerry had his head in his hands, but he leaped to answer the phone when it rang. He listened grimly for a while.

"I have to tell you," we heard him say, "that now's not the time for us to deal with Case's school problems, Mr. Hayes."

Mr. Hayes, my principal! I'd forgotten all about the trouble I was in at school. This morning was ancient times.

"Let me explain," Gerry said more loudly into the receiver. "My—our—baby is missing. She may have been kidnapped."

That ended the phone call fast.

"Case," Gerry said, "how can you be so very very good and so very very bad all at the same time?"

"What now?" Mother asked him.

"I wasn't bad," I protested. "I made a party for our student teacher, and the gym window got broken. I didn't break it—some hoods did. But now I'm not allowed in English class anymore."

"Stop!" Mother put her hand out. "I can't cope with another thing now."

Gerry took off to check the hospitals personally. Mother called the police to make sure they were actively searching for Meredith and to ask about calling in the FBI or hiring private investigators. After she got off the phone, I asked her what they'd told her, but she just frowned at me and said, "Whatever you do, don't tell Grams *anything,* if she calls before we get Meredith back."

"*If* we get Meredith back," Jen murmured.

"Jen!" Mother shrieked.

Sometime around midnight Jen and I went to bed.

"Want to sleep with me?" she asked.

"Yes, thanks."

"It's not just for you," she said. "It's for me. I feel so awful about Meredith. You were right about Charlene. You were right all along, and we should have listened to you."

Being right was no fun at the moment. "At least Charlene's taking good care of her, wherever they are," I said. I'd said it before, but I needed to hear it again. "I want Merry back so bad."

"You think Charlene plans to keep our baby?"

"I think she's going to pretend Meredith's hers."

"But why didn't she just have her own instead of stealing ours, if she wanted one so badly?" Jen asked.

"Maybe she couldn't. Maybe she had a baby and lost it. Who knows?"

"Not me. I didn't like that woman enough to want to get to know her."

"You never said you didn't like her."

"Well, I didn't want to encourage you, because you were so against her. I'm sorry, Case. I should have listened to you, but I was just glad to have the house quiet again."

"I wonder if she planned to steal Merry right from the beginning," I said, thinking out loud. "I wonder if that's what she took the job for."

"That's crazy. How could she think she could get away with it?"

"How do we know how Charlene thinks? I bet you she believes that Merry would be better off with her, because she loves her more than we do. Because Mother works and I was jealous."

"Oh, you were not," Jen said.

"Yes, I was, but I'm not anymore."

"Case, even if you were a little jealous, you still loved Meredith. *I* didn't care about her at all. To me she was just a pest who screamed all the time."

"Don't talk about her in the past tense," I said. "She's still ours. We'll get her back."

"I hope so," Jen said. Sighing, she turned over to go to sleep.

I expected to stay awake all night because I felt so bad, but next thing I knew it was Friday morning. I guess thinking tires you out, and I was thinking hard, sifting through my memory bank for clues. I woke up with one in my head: the peanut butter container from the natural foods store. The police might not be as quick to dismiss the natural foods store idea as Mother had been. I got up and called the station.

Sergeant Cullen wasn't due in until later, they told me. So I gave my clue to the officer who answered the phone. She said she'd relay the message.

Half an hour later, Mother and Gerry left to go badger the police about doing more to find their child. Jen went to school. She said even school had to be better than sitting home feeling helpless.

"What are you going to do?" she asked me.

"I don't know yet," I told her. But I had to do something to help find Meredith. Sitting around feeling helpless wasn't my thing, either.

·THIRTEEN·

Today was Friday, the seventh grade's Field Day. Since I wasn't allowed to participate in the events, thanks to Mrs. Thompson, I couldn't have picked a better time to skip school and search for my baby sister. Willie could participate in Field Day, but I doubted he'd want to. I took a chance and called him.

"Willie, would you rather play volleyball or help me track down Meredith?"

"They didn't find her yet? That means she's really been kidnapped. Wow!"

I didn't give him time to absorb the shock. "What I want to do is talk to those ladies in the park again," I said. "I just bet Charlene told them more about herself than she ever told us."

"Ummm. Okay, I guess I can fake a stomachache once in my life. My mother won't want me to go to Field Day with a stomachache." He hung up, leaving me surprised. I'd expected getting Willie to play hooky would be harder.

A minute later he called back and said, "Be there as soon as I finish breakfast."

I was on my doorstep waiting impatiently for him

when he arrived at eight. "I couldn't leave until my parents went to work," he explained.

He had his bike. No need for me to leave a note, since my parents thought I was going to school. I got my bike, and we pedaled off to the park.

Nobody was on the bench outside Tiny Tot Playground. "It's too early," Willie said. "They probably come only in the afternoon."

I hadn't thought of that, but I had another idea. "Okay, then meanwhile we can check out natural foods stores in the area. Let's find a telephone book. I wish I'd looked in the yellow pages before we left. We can call around and maybe find out where Charlene shopped."

"There's a natural foods store near here, you know," Willie said. "Want to try it?" I'd forgotten Willie knew the area better than I did. "Or maybe we should leave that for the police," he added, with some of his usual caution.

"They might not think it's important, Willie. Listen, it's probably the wrong store, but I have to do *something*. We can buy some granola there, okay? I'm hungry."

Dutifully Willie led me to a little, old-fashioned, wood-shingled house. The edge of its wraparound porch was just visible from the main street of our town. We left our bikes on the porch. Bins and sacks and shelves full of labeled foodstuffs filled what once must have been the living and dining rooms downstairs. In the hall, I stood beside a display of fancy teas and thought I heard a baby cry.

Seeing me misty-eyed and frozen, Willie whispered, "I'll ask for the granola."

"I don't have any money with me," I whispered back.

"Don't worry. I'm loaded."

All of a sudden, tears were sliding down my cheeks. I hadn't cried last night about losing my baby sister, but now the flow wouldn't stop. Since I couldn't ask questions about Charlene very casually while I was bawling, I told Willie to go ahead, and I stood back waiting and wiping my face dry.

A sturdy woman with a thick braid of dark hair was stacking soy milk containers on a shelf. I liked her easy smile when she looked up at Willie's approach and her throaty voice when she answered him about the granola. "There's boxed, or we have our own mix. Why don't you taste that? It's good."

"Yeah, Charlene says it is," Willie, my clever Willie, said.

"Charlene?" the woman repeated, alert suddenly.

"Yeah, she buys her stuff here, doesn't she?"

"I don't usually know my customers' names," the woman said. Stiffly, she pointed. "That aisle has the bins with the cereals. The granola's the end one."

Willie hesitated, opened his mouth, closed it, and then just thanked her and disappeared down the aisle. The woman stared after him intently.

A funny prickling began at the back of my neck, and without even knowing I was going to do it, I called out, "Ina!"

Her head jerked around.

I moved to where she could see me better. "Ina's your name, isn't it?" I asked.

"Who are you?" she demanded.

"I'm Case. Charlene must have told you about me. She works for my family."

"Oh," the woman, Ina—I was sure it was Ina—said. "You're one of the girls Charlene was baby-sitting for? She didn't mention a boy." Ina looked after Willie.

"Willie's my friend," I said. "I just have two sisters, an older one and a baby."

"Yes." Ina gave me a big smile. "Charlene was crazy about that baby. It's too bad she had to quit the job. Are your parents going to look for another sitter?"

"I guess so," I said. "Do you know where she went?"

"Charlene?" Ina looked at me more closely. "Why do you want to know?"

"My mother wants to talk to her."

Ina shook her head. "Charlene didn't tell me where she was going. . . . Do you want to buy something?"

She sounded less friendly. I didn't want to make her suspicious before the police could question her; so I just smiled and said, "Willie's buying the granola." He came back and paid for half a pound of the mix in a paper bag. It was expensive.

"I guess we didn't find out anything there," he said when we were reclaiming our bikes outside the store.

"Oh, yes, we did," I told him. "That was Ina, Charlene's friend."

A detached garage was set back to one side of the house. "I'm going to see if the pickup's in there, Willie."

"You are? I'm coming with you."

"No, you go call the police. Tell them to get here in a hurry."

He hesitated, then shrugged and took off on his bike. I left mine against a tree. I wasn't absolutely sure Ina knew where Charlene and Meredith were, but my hunch was she did.

Before I got much past the corner of the house, the back door opened and Ina demanded, "Where do you think you're going?"

"I'm just walking," I said, "taking a shortcut."

"To where? You get out of here." She sounded *very* unfriendly now.

"You must like her a lot to help her kidnap a baby, Ina," I said.

"What are you talking about?"

"Charlene has my baby sister. Where did she take her?"

Ina shook her head as if she didn't understand something. She said, "You're not from the family Charlene baby-sat for, are you? *He* sent you, didn't he? Charlene's stepfather. You're one of *his* kids." She took a step toward me, her thick braid swinging. "Well, you can tell him he had no right to make her give her baby up, and now she's got it back, she's gonna keep it. You and your daddy ought to be ashamed of yourselves. You're driving that poor girl crazy. Don't you realize that baby's all she's got?"

"That baby's not hers," I protested. "Merry's our baby. She's my sister."

"Charlene gave birth to her. The baby's hers." Ina folded her arms and stood there on guard. "You go back and tell him I'll go to court if I have to, to testify that she's a fit mother. He thinks he can do what he wants because my aunt deserted her, but she's got me to help her now. I'll stand behind her."

"The baby?" I asked, bewildered.

"Both of them, my cousin Charlene *and* her baby."

I went back to what I understood. "But that's not Charlene's baby," I insisted. "Charlene stole Merry. You've got to believe me! She was baby-sitting for us and she stole *our* baby."

Suddenly Ina's eyes widened. Her hand went to her mouth. Then as cautiously as if she were exploring new territory, she began to speak. "She said she was quitting the baby-sitting job so that she could get her baby back. . . . Yesterday . . . yesterday she drove home to upstate New York. She said she had a plan to take her baby back without being seen—her baby, her own baby, from the family her stepfather sold it to. She. . . ."

For a long moment we stood there staring at each other. I could see Ina's alarm as she began to realize whose baby Charlene had taken.

"But if she didn't drive home, she could've . . . That baby . . ." Ina whispered, "Oh, my God!"

"Let me speak to Charlene," I said. "You'll see I'm telling the truth."

157

"I can't do that. I can't."

"Then you're still willing to help her kidnap my baby sister?"

"Kidnap? Oh, no!" Ina said. She made a fist and pressed her knuckles against her lips. Words poured out as if she couldn't help herself. "Charlene said it was her baby, her own child, the one he made her give up. And I told her I'd help her because he'd treated her so bad, and she never had a chance after her mother ran off. . . . Oh, my God!"

"She's here?" I asked.

Ina came to suddenly and said, "They're upstairs. I'll go." She stopped and turned around to explain, "I wanted to help her. I thought someone had to be good to her."

"Did you get her the job with the agency?" I asked in a sudden burst of inspiration.

"Sure. She didn't have any experience, except for raising her stepbrothers and sisters, and she was scared to apply for any other kind of job. So when the agency called to ask if I was free, I sent her in my place. Then I told the agency that the family said they'd already hired someone else. I thought I was doing everybody a good deed, except the agency, maybe." Ina shook her head and disappeared into the house.

I followed her inside and listened. A minute later I heard someone upstairs screaming, "No, no, no, no!" I found the staircase and was halfway up it when the police arrived.

*   *   *

158

Mother and Gerry let me hold my baby sister in the car going home from the police station. I was the heroine. Even Mother had said so, and Sergeant Cullen had offered to make me an honorary detective. Well, he'd been joking, but in all the heavy drama at the police station, it had been nice to have something to laugh about.

Merry was sound asleep. She'd been making a fuss, which wasn't surprising. Charlene had started screaming like a maniac when the police took Merry away from her, but Merry seemed fine. They'd handed her to me and bundled Charlene into a squad car with Ina, who had to go along with them for questioning. Once we got to the police station, Charlene and Ina were taken somewhere, and I delivered Meredith to my parents, who were waiting there for me. That was really something. We were all crying so hard nobody could hear Meredith yelling. The police didn't keep us long. Sergeant Cullen said we should all go home and rest, and that was when he made the remark about hiring me as a detective.

"Who knows what she'll become!" Mother said. "With Case, one can never tell."

Right after that, we got into our own car with me in the back holding Meredith on my lap. That was illegal, but none of us was willing to let her out of our arms. Merry quieted down then. I know I'm telling this in circles, but we really were spinning by the end of that morning.

Anyway, while Gerry drove us home, I had to go over what Ina had told me again because they still didn't understand why Charlene had taken our baby.

"Probably it looked like her own. Because Merry's blue-eyed and blond like Charlene. It could even be that she took a baby-sitting job so as to find a baby to replace the one they took away from her."

Would you believe, Mother listened to me and nodded respectfully? "I suppose that's possible," she said.

Then they talked about how incredible it was, especially that it had happened to us, because it was the kind of thing you read about in the paper, happening to other people. Gerry said about three times, "We should have listened to you, Case. You were the one who spotted that Charlene was disturbed."

"That she was weird," I said. "I don't know if she's really crazy."

"Who knows?" Mother said. "She must be to think she could get away with kidnapping."

Mother suggested we drive to the pediatrician and have Meredith checked over, but Gerry thought that could wait. "She seems fine," he said. "Let her sleep."

We got to our own driveway, and Gerry said, "Case, anything you want, you name it."

"Anything?" I asked.

"Anything," Mother said, smiling at me over the back of the front seat. But being Mother, she added, "Almost."

To have them at my feet was a new experience. I nuzzled my baby sister and considered. What did I want? Basically, I had what I wanted, which was Merry back home and all of us together. But it'd be stupid to turn down the opportunity of a lifetime, wouldn't it? Anything I wanted—it was sort of like having three wishes where the last wish has to be to make things the way they were before. I'd better be careful.

"First of all," I said, "do you think you could make Mrs. Thompson let me out of solitary for the rest of the term?"

"You bet," Mother said. "I'll tackle that one. I'll even ask her to apologize to you if you want."

I imagined Mrs. Thompson on bended knees telling me how she had never really appreciated me, and how now she knew she just hadn't recognized true genius when she saw it. "No, thanks, Mother," I said. "Just letting me back in class will do." After all, I *had* gone around bending rules all year, which was rough on a teacher who believed in them the way Mrs. Thompson did.

"What else?" Gerry asked. "I'd like to buy you something."

"I could use some swim goggles," I said, thinking about the summer coming up and all the time we were going to spend at the pool. "And maybe a new bathing suit."

"Is that all?" Gerry laughed.

"You know what'd really be good?" I added. "If you let me baby-sit Merry this summer, like maybe half a day a few days a week."

"And pay you for it. Sure," Gerry said. "That means we have to find someone to fill in part-time only, which would work out well. What else?"

161

I couldn't think of anything, but there they were looking at me, eager to do something to show how grateful they were; so I joked, "How about a plaque? We could hang it in the kitchen, and then when you get mad at me, you could look at it and remember how good I am."

That made Mother laugh, and she suggested, "It could say, 'No matter how it seems, remember the kid means well.'"

"How about just, 'Case is a terrific kid'?" Gerry put in quickly.

"I like that better," I said.

"Case, you know we love you very much," Mother said seriously.

"Even when I'm impossible?"

"Even then."

"Good," I said. "Let's put that on the plaque, too, so nobody forgets it."

I was thinking about neatness and how much better I'd gotten at it, thanks to Charlene. Probably I'd been wrong to believe neatness was something you were born with. Well, it's always nice to learn something new.

My baby sister woke up then and began crowing at me, telling me how proud she was of me, of course.

"Hey, munchkin! Hey, little buddy," I told her. "I love you, too."

C. S. ADLER was born in New York City and attended Hunter College High School and Hunter College. She has a master's degree in education from Russell Sage College. For more than seven years she taught English in a middle school in Niskayuna, New York, where she and her husband raised three sons and now live.

Her first novel for young people, *The Magic of the Glits,* won the 1979 Golden Kite Award for fiction and the 1982 William Allen White Children's Book Award. She has since published a number of acclaimed novels for children and young adults, including *If You Need Me, Split Sisters, With Westie and the Tin Man,* and *Roadside Valentine.*